PRINCE VALIANT

Special thanks to the SPECIAL COLLECTIONS RESEARCH CENTER of the SYRACUSE UNIVERSITY LIBRARY for providing the scans for the vast majority of the *Prince Valiant* strips, reproduced from original syndicate proof sheets, in this volume. Visit their website at http://library.syr.edu/find/scrc/

Prince Valiant Vol. 13: 1961–1962 Fantagraphics Books, Inc. 7563 Lake City Way NE, Seattle, WA 98115. Edited by Brian M. Kane. Editorial Liaison: Gary Groth. Series design by Adam Grano. Production by Michael Heck. Restoration by Paul Baresh. Associate Publisher: Eric Reynolds. Publisher: Gary Groth. All comics material © 2016 King Features Syndicate. This edition copyright © 2016 Fantagraphics Books, Inc. "We Are All the Sum of the Stories We Have Been Told" and Prince Valiant tryout/illustration art © 2016 Charles Vess. "Hal Foster's Advertising Art: Home and Hearth" © 2016 Brian M. Kane. All images and photographs by and of Hal Foster and his family in "We are All the Sum of the Stories we Have Been Told" and "Hal Foster's Advertising Art: Home and Hearth" copyright © 2016 The Harold R. Foster Estate. All rights reserved. Permission to quote or reproduce material for reviews or notices must be obtained from Fantagraphics Books, Inc. in writing, at 7563 Lake City Way NE, Seattle, WA 98115. First edition: June 2016 ISBN: 978-1-60699-925-7. Library of Congress Control Number: 2015960915. Printed in China.

PRINCE VALIANT

VOL. 13: 1961-1962 — BY HAL FOSTER

PUBLISHED BY FANTAGRAPHICS BOOKS, INC., SEATTLE.

Harold R. Foster's
Prince Valiant
IN THE DAYS OF KING ARTHUR
Illustrated by Charles Vess

OUR STORY: YUAN CHEN'S MESSAGE FROM THE EMPEROR OF THE MIDDLE KINGDOM IS A TONIC FOR THE WARRIORS OF CAMELOT: IT PROMISES ADVENTURE AND EXCITEMENT AND A CHANCE FOR GLORY. KING ARTHUR CONVENES THE ROUND TABLE. "THE LAST OF THE ANCIENT SPICE ROUTES HAS BEEN SEVERED BY THE HUNS AND THEIR ALLIES."

"THE EMPOROR PROPOSES A TREATY: A SHARE OF THE SPICE REVENUES IN RETURN FOR FINDING-- AND PROTECTING-- A NEW SPICE ROUTE."

AND WHO WILL LEAD THE QUEST? KING ARTHUR TURNS AS HE SO OFTEN HAS TO PRINCE VALIANT. "HAND PICK YOUR MEN AND COME BACK TO ME WITH A PLAN. WE MUST START AT ONCE." VAL SPENDS A DAY WITH YUAN CHEN AND HIS MAPS.

IT IS A DAZZLING PROSPECT. AT LAST THE KING WILL HAVE THE MONEY HE NEEDS TO FINISH THE REBUILDING OF HIS KINGDOM, RUINED BY MORDRED'S RULE. HIS OLD FRAME IS STRENGTHENED BY UNEXPECTED HOPE.

SOON A PLAN FORMS IN HIS HEAD. HE SAYS TO YUAN CHEN: "THE OLD SPICE ROUTES CROSSED THE DESERT WHERE CARAVANS WERE VULNERABLE TO BOTH THE HUNS AND THE WEATHER. LET US OPEN A NOTHERN ROUTE. RIVERS WILL CARRY US MOST OF THE WAY."

BY LAND AND SEA COURIERS CARRY A MESSAGE FROM KING ARTHUR TO THE EMPEROR OF THE MIDDLE KINGDOM: "WE ARE WITH YOU."
NEXT WEEK: BON VOYAGE

WE ARE ALL THE SUM OF THE STORIES WE HAVE BEEN TOLD

Foreword by Charles Vess

As a young boy I eagerly fed on the pulp-infused fiction that was *Tarzan of the Apes* and *John Carter of Mars*. The grand adventures of Flash Gordon, Spider-Man, The Fantastic Four and Conan the Barbarian dominated my youthful imagination. As I grew a few years older, those simple, war-soaked tales were leavened by Ray Bradbury's quieter, poetic visions. Soon after, my discovery of J.R.R. Tolkien's *The Lord of the Rings* left me longing to wander again through worlds made with that same sense of wonder and magic.

Then, in my late teens and early twenties, I discovered a series of novels edited by Lin Carter and published under *The Sign of the Unicorn* through Ballantine Books. His perceptive editorial choices introduced me to the writings of Lord Dunsany, James Branch Cabell, Evangeline Walton and Hope Mirrlees. Almost at the same time I became aware of Golden Age illustrators Aubrey Beardsley, Arthur Rackham, Howard Pyle, N.C. Wyeth and Maxfield Parrish. Together they were a perfect storm of art and writing that changed my aesthetic life forever.

As one grows older, it's interesting to note which artists and writers whose work had once completely enthralled you fall away. The pantheon of art gods that I clutched so defiantly to my breast during art school in my twenties is rather different from those whom I look to these days for inspiration. Now in my mid-sixties, the magical spell once cast over me by Alex Raymond, Jack Kirby, Frank Frazetta and Parrish has lost much of its luster. Not that I would ever dismiss those artists or others of the same high caliber, but their work no longer creates the same sudden frisson of desire to run to my drawing board and draw as it once did. And perhaps that's as it should be? Certainly as you grow and mature as a person, so should your interests in art and literature.

Of course, it's just as interesting to acknowledge which of those early inspirations still walk close by your side, choosing now

Opposite: *Charles Vess drew this* Prince Valiant *tryout page in 2003. It depicts the March 15, 1987 strip (Page #2614), and Brian Kane colored it. A black-and-white version appeared in* The Definitive Prince Valiant Companion *on page #38.*

and again to whisper a bit of sage advice in your ear—advice that you might have ignored when you were consumed with the eagerness of youth. Tolkien, Bradbury, Dunsany, Walton, Rackham, Mucha and Pyle (joined later by John Bauer and Herman Vogel) are some that, to this day, have remained close friends.

And—of course—Hal Foster.

I grew up in the 1950s and '60s reading his glorious strip, *Prince Valiant*. Every week, right there in the pages of my hometown Sunday newspaper, it appeared, enthralling me in equal part with its epic adventures that sprawled across far distant, exotic lands—as well as the subtle intricacies of Val's domestic life with his wife Aleta and their family.

I still have a long, late 1960s run of the strip that I pulled from the paper. Carefully clipping each individual panel, I put them into spiral-bound notebooks. I look at them occasionally, yellowed now with age and discolored by an excess of tape. When I turn those pages I'm right there again, lying on the carpet in my family's living room, reading them for the first time. A long afternoon of play stretches ahead of me, but not before I thoroughly study this week's new installment of my favorite comic strip.

So when I reread it today, there is always a soft patina of nostalgia that welcomes me; but if that were all there were to be gleaned from those carefully preserved pages, Hal Foster's work would have already joined those other "fallen" heroes of my youth.

As the years roll on, I find that every time I dip back into any of the multiple iterations of reprints that line my bookshelves there is still so much more to learn from Foster's work. I learned from all the care, thought and research that he applied to his stories. With varying degrees of success I have tried,

in my own art, to recreate the certainty that if I could somehow walk past the borders of any of his panels I would continue out into a lush and ever-expanding world. If you pay as much attention as I have to the manner in which he carefully delineated the hills, forests, rocks and rivers that densely populate his tale, you would have to agree that each of those elements are as important to the story he is telling as the human characters that nominally carry his plot forward. No landscape or architectural element is used to merely fill up space in his backgrounds—they actively add a unique narrative depth and impetus to Foster's compelling tale.

For instance, a bleak landscape with its tortured trees standing sentinel to a particularly gloomy castle where his latest villain might live tells us as much about that character's mindset as Foster's well-chosen words, perhaps even more. Too, the emotional state of every horse, dog—or any animal, really, that he put into his narrative—is as carefully defined as the individual expressions drawn on each character's face or the gestures of their hands.

A tree in one landscape is never mindlessly repeated in another—each is distinctive and belongs to that particular environment, whether his story is taking place in Norway, the Mediterranean or across the North American storm-tossed sea.

Every one of those visual elements share equal importance with the human actors that play out their lives on Foster's dynamic storytelling stage. Speaking of those pen-and-ink actors, I think I'd like to dispel a current notion that seems to be making the rounds. According to some, the more simply drawn characters are, the easier it is for a reader to identify with them. Ha! By that way of thinking, I should never have identified so strongly with Val & Co., nor for that matter with Pogo or Flash Gordon or The Phantom, or...well, the list could go on and on. I believe that the much more important factor is whether or not the story you are reading is personally compelling to you. And even after all these years the story of the Singing Sword is infinitely compelling, both in its narrative and in the morality of its principle players. I have a suspicion that I would not be the person I am today without the lessons I absorbed—without even being aware of it—from Hal Foster's creation. Our world would certainly be a better place with more people with simple, noble hearts like Prince Valiant—and far fewer slinking villains like Mordred inhabiting its corridors of power—wouldn't it?

I'd like to relate two instances from my own life as a professional illustrator that brought me in close contact with Hal Foster and his creation. In the early 1990s, Marvel Comics acquired the licensing rights to four comic strips owned by the King Features Syndicate, and *Prince Valiant* was one of them. When I was asked to write and draw a four-issue miniseries for them, my heart leapt at the thought. But immediately I knew that with each individual issue clocking in at forty-eight pages, unless the powers that be were willing to wait a VERY long time indeed, that I shouldn't and couldn't produce the art. But I did say yes to the writing so I got busy with my research, rereading every strip (what a lovely, lovely chore that was!), including all of the newer ones written or drawn since Foster's retirement: incorporating characters and elements from those stories as well. I was very

pleased with my own efforts (and with Elaine Lee's polishing of my lengthy outlines) but unfortunately, in the manner of these things, deadlines got tighter and tighter and production values fell by the wayside—leaving only the gorgeous painted covers by my friend Michael Kaluta to shine as they were meant to.

I did receive a very encouraging letter from Jay Kennedy, the editor of the strip at King Features, and soon after he called with an offer I almost couldn't resist. In 2003, more than sixty years after the strip had begun, and twenty-five years after Hal Foster's successor had started drawing the page, John Cullen Murphy was beginning to think seriously of his own retirement. Casting about for a replacement, Kennedy asked if I would produce a tryout page. Reflecting on that moment now, I'm certain that more artists than just I were asked the same. Anyway, thrilled (and completely intimidated!) I started to work. Given only a week to produce the art my days at the

drawing board were long, and the nights even longer still. All that effort paid off, because I was subsequently offered the job. Upon much hard reflection, though, I said no. Perhaps if the newspaper page today still looked as it had in its Sunday comics prime, I would have chosen otherwise. But with its once full-page glory reduced by the severe restrictions imposed by the few newspapers that still carried it, I knew that I wouldn't be happy seeing my work jammed into a corner slot of the sadly reduced Sunday comics, sometimes without even the use of color. Happily for those of us that remain fans of the strip, the artists that did say yes (Gary Gianni, Mark Schultz and now Thomas Yeates) have all done an excellent job of carrying forward the legacy of Prince Valiant, and we should all thank them for their diligent work.

Enjoy your reading of this amazing collection; its like will not come again.

Right: Title page illustration for the Marvel Select Prince Valiant *series (1994); it appeared in all four issues.*

Opposite: Back cover illustration for issue #1 of the Marvel Select Prince Valiant *series (1994).*

This is the first panel of the August 20, 1944 Prince Valiant strip (Page #39), reproduced at its original size (see Prince Valiant Vol. 4: 1943–1944 for the color version). It is from the private collection of Charles Vess.

Prince Valiant
IN THE DAYS OF KING ARTHUR
WRITTEN AND ILLUSTRATED BY HAROLD R FOSTER

Our Story: THE STORM WENT CRASHING BY INTO THE DISTANCE. AT LAST PRINCE VALIANT SHUDDERS AND TURNS OVER TO LET THE RAIN SOOTHE HIS EYES SEARED BY THE BLINDING FLASH OF THE THUNDERBOLT.

WHEN SIGHT RETURNS HE SEES THE SHATTERED STUMP THAT RECEIVED THE FULL FORCE OF THE BOLT. SOMETHING GLITTERS AMIDST THE RUIN.

THRASOS HAS AT LAST FOUND A HIDING PLACE WHERE HE IS SAFE FROM THE VENGEANCE OF HIS PURSUER ...... FOREVERMORE.

BACK IN THE CITY MANY CRISES HAVE TO BE MET. ALTHOUGH THE WAR IS OVER, THE PRISONERS STILL OUTNUMBER THE CITIZENS. NIGHT HAS FALLEN ERE VAL HAS SOLVED ALL HIS PROBLEMS.

HE HASTENS TO ALETA'S APARTMENT, ONLY TO BE BARRED FROM SEEING HER BY THE LADIES IN WAITING.

THEN KATWIN PARTS THE CURTAINS, CALM AND COMPETENT, THOUGH LITTLE LINES OF ANXIETY MARK HER BROW AND MOUTH. SHE SMILES REASSURINGLY AT VAL AND VANISHES.

VAL PACES THE CORRIDOR, FORGETFUL OF HIS ORDEAL IN THE FACE OF ANOTHER, A GREATER ONE.....

1247.   1-1-61

AT LAST SERVANTS COAX HIM OUT OF HIS WET ARMOR AND INTO A DRY ROBE. AT DAWN HE FINDS FITFUL REST. ALONE.

NEXT WEEK- From the Shadows

Prince Valiant

IN THE DAYS OF KING ARTHUR

WRITTEN AND ILLUSTRATED BY HAROLD R FOSTER

Our Story: A SERVANT ROUSES PRINCE VALIANT FROM HIS WEARY STUPOR. THE LADIES IN WAITING HAVE GONE, THE CORRIDOR IS EMPTY AND MORNING HAS COME.

THE WASHBASIN AND COMB RESTORE VAL'S VANITY (NO SMALL THING AMONG YOUNG MEN OF HIS AGE).

ALETA, QUEEN OF THE MISTY ISLES, CALLS IN HER HANDMAIDENS TO DO THEIR BEST, FOR HER MAN MUST NOT KNOW OF THE ORDEAL THAT HAD TAKEN HER SO CLOSE TO THE EDGE OF THE SHADOWS.

VAL ENTERS AND FEELS THAT OLD FAMILIAR CATCH AT HIS HEART. BUT ALL THE COSMETICS IN THE WORLD COULD NOT DISGUISE THE FACT THAT THE WING OF DEATH HAS BRUSHED HIS BELOVED DANGEROUSLY CLOSE.

AND NOW ALETA HAS TWO BABIES TO COMFORT. *"THE SHOCK OF THRASOS' ATTACK ALMOST ACCOMPLISHED WHAT HIS SWORD COULD NOT,"* MURMURS VAL. *"HIS DEATH WAS LIKE DIVINE JUSTICE!"*

HERALDS GO OUT INTO THE CITY AND PROCLAIM THE GOOD NEWS. *"THIS DAY A PRINCE IS BORN TO THE ROYAL FAMILY OF THE MISTY ISLES!"*

IT IS NICE TO BE LOVED, BUT WITH A BABY ON ONE ARM AND A HUSBAND HOLDING TIGHTLY ON THE OTHER FOR HOURS, WHAT IS A QUEEN TO DO IF HER NOSE ITCHES? SHE SENDS VAL BACK TO WORK.

OUT IN THE SUNSHINE, WITH HIS HEAD IN THE CLOUDS, STANDS THE MOST USELESS THING IN THE WORLD, A PROUD NEW FATHER!

NEXT WEEK- **Prince Arn Abdicates.**

1248.   1-8-61

Prince Valiant
IN THE DAYS OF KING ARTHUR

WRITTEN AND ILLUSTRATED BY Harold R Foster

Our Story: PRINCE VALIANT WANDERS AIMLESSLY, HIS HEAD AND HEART FILLED WITH PLANS FOR HIS NEW SON'S GLORIOUS FUTURE. IT WILL BE SOME TIME BEFORE HE CAN GET DOWN TO SERIOUS WORK.

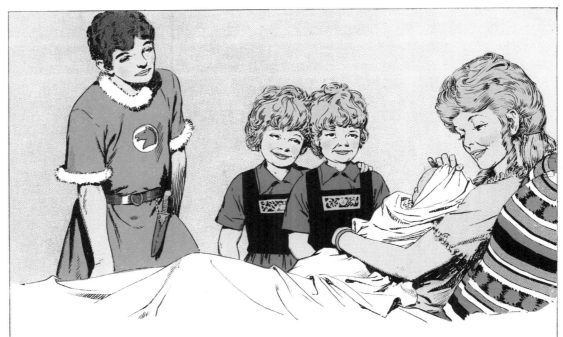

PRINCE ARN AND THE TWINS ARE INTRODUCED TO THEIR NEW BROTHER. ARN IS QUITE SERIOUS AS HE LOOKS DOWN ON HIS RIVAL. UP TO NOW HE HAS BEEN SOLE HEIR TO THE THRONES OF TWO KINGDOMS, THULE AND THE MISTY ISLES.

THE TWINS SIZE UP THE NEW ARRIVAL ACCORDING TO THEIR NATURE. THINKS VALETA: "I WILL CHARM HIM AND MAKE HIM MY VERY OWN PET." KAREN PLANS THUS: "A BOY, HAH, HE WILL BE VERY IMPORTANT AND SPOILED, BUT I'LL SHOW HIM WHO IS BOSS AROUND HERE."

PRINCE ARN IS, AS USUAL, FOLLOWED EVERYWHERE BY COURTIERS AND GUARDS. HE FEELS VERY IMPORTANT. THEN HE SEES LADS HIS OWN AGE PLAYING FREE AND UNRESTRAINED. HE MAKES A DECISION.

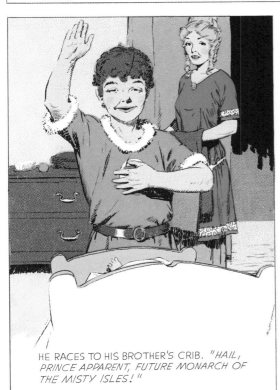

HE RACES TO HIS BROTHER'S CRIB. "HAIL, PRINCE APPARENT, FUTURE MONARCH OF THE MISTY ISLES!"

AND AN HOUR LATER HE IS WITH PAUL AND DIANE PREPARING A SEAFOOD DINNER ON THE BEACH AS THEY USED TO DO WHEN HE WAS HERE LAST.

THE PRISONERS OF WAR ARE PUT TO WORK FINISHING THE WORK ON THE WALLS. THEY HAVE BEEN DISARMED BUT HAVE BUILDER'S TOOLS.....AND THEY PLOT.

NEXT WEEK – Freedom!

1249.   1-15-61

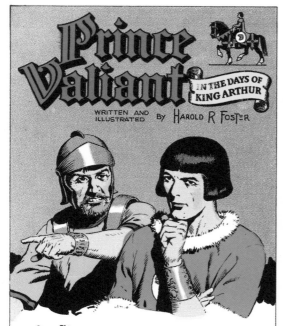

Prince Valiant
IN THE DAYS OF KING ARTHUR
WRITTEN AND ILLUSTRATED BY HAROLD R FOSTER

Our Story : WHEN PRINCE VALIANT LEARNS THAT THE LARGE HOST OF PRISONERS OF WAR WORKING ON THE FORTIFICATIONS ARE GETTING RESTLESS AND PLAN REVOLT, HE IS PREPARED. HE SENDS FOR BOLTAR.

THE REVOLT COMES JUST IN TIME, FOR THE NORTHMEN HAVE BEEN IDLE TOO LONG AND ARE CONTINUALLY GETTING INTO TROUBLE. THEY PUT IN A GOOD DAY'S WORK.

AN ENTERTAINMENT, QUITE FAMILIAR IN THESE TIMES, IS STAGED IN FULL VIEW OF THE PRISONERS. A FEW HOTHEADS ARE COOLED OFF, AND FOR A WHILE THERE IS NO MORE TROUBLE.

FOR CENTURIES THE MISTY ISLES HAVE KNOWN ONLY PEACE AND FREEDOM. NOW EACH ISLET IS CROWNED WITH A GRIM FORTRESS, FOR IN THESE CHANGING TIMES ONLY THE STRONG CAN BE FREE.

ENJOYING THEIR FREEDOM TO THE UTMOST ARE ARN, PAUL AND DIANE. THE CARES OF THE WORLD ARE FAR AWAY AS THEY FROLIC ON THE BEACH AND COOK ENORMOUS QUANTITIES OF SHELL-FISH AND FISH BY THEIR SECRET CAVE.

AND THERE ARE THREE OTHERS WHO DESIRE FREEDOM SO FIERCELY THAT THEY ARE WILLING TO RISK DEATH FOR IT.

NEXT WEEK - **Captured**

1250.

1 - 22 - 61

Prince Valiant

IN THE DAYS OF KING ARTHUR

WRITTEN AND ILLUSTRATED BY Harold R. Foster

Our Story: THREE DESPERATE MEN CREEP THROUGH THE DARK, PRISONERS OF WAR RISKING LIFE FOR LIBERTY. THEIR PLANS HAVE BEEN CAREFULLY LAID.

IN A COVE WHERE FISHING CRAFT ARE MOORED, ONE WHO CAN SWIM IS SENT TO STEAL A BOAT.

THE OTHER TWO FIND A CAVE AND WAIT. WAIT, WHILE FEAR AND ANXIETY MAKE THEM EVEN MORE DESPERATE AND DANGEROUS.

SUNUP, AND DOWN THE CLIFF COME ARN, PAUL AND DIANE, EAGER FOR A DAY OF FISHING, COOKING, EATING, EXPLORING AND, OF COURSE, EATING AGAIN.

WHEN A SWIM IS SUGGESTED, DIANE GOES OFF TO HER OWN PRIVATE BEACH. THE BOYS LOOK AT EACH OTHER IN SURPRISE, DIANE HAS BLUSHED! SHE IS GROWING UP! THEY ARE NO LONGER CHILDREN!

THE THREE YOUNG PEOPLE ARE PUZZLED TO SEE A BOAT PUT IN TO THE BEACH THEY CLAIM AS THEIR OWN. BUT THERE IS EVEN A GREATER SURPRISE IN STORE.

1251.

THEY ARE SEIZED ROUGHLY AND DRAGGED INTO THE CAVE.

NEXT WEEK - Kidnapped!

1-29-61

Prince Valiant
IN THE DAYS OF KING ARTHUR
WRITTEN AND ILLUSTRATED BY HAROLD R FOSTER

Our Story: PRINCE ARN AND HIS PLAYMATES FALL INTO THE HANDS OF THE ESCAPED PRISONERS. THE DESPERATE MEN MUST MAKE A CHOICE FOR THEIR OWN SAFETY; WILL THEY KILL THE CHILDREN OR TAKE THEM ALONG?

" I AM PRINCE ARN, SON OF QUEEN ALETA; UNHAND ME, OR MY SIRE, PRINCE VALIANT WILL SEARCH THE WIDE SEAS TO BRING YOU TO JUSTICE."

ARN'S WORDS SETTLE THE QUESTION. A PRINCE WILL MAKE A HOSTAGE FOR THEIR SAFETY AND BRING A HUGE RANSOM. THEY ROW OUT TO SEA.

WITHOUT FOOD OR WATER THE DAY SEEMS ENDLESS, BUT AT DUSK A LONELY LIGHT ON A SMALL ISLAND PROMISES RELIEF.

ARN, DIANE AND PAUL ARE BOUND AND GAGGED, AND THE THREE FUGITIVES CREEP TOWARD A FISHERMAN'S COTTAGE.

THERE COMES THE SOUND OF SUDDEN CON-FLICT, A WOMAN SCREAMS.....THEN SILENCE. WHEN THEY RETURN THERE IS BLOOD ON THEIR HANDS AND THEY ARE LOADED WITH PLUNDER.

FOOD IS PREPARED AND THE SCRAPS THROWN TO THE CHILDREN. DAY FINDS THEM SAILING, BUT NO ONE KNOWS WHERE.

NEXT WEEK—Evidence.

1252.

2-5-61

Our Story: THREE ESCAPED PRISONERS STEAL A BOAT, AND IN A DESPERATE BID FOR FREEDOM, HOLD PRINCE ARN AND HIS COMPANIONS AS HOSTAGES AND FOR RANSOM.

PRINCE VALIANT AND ALETA ARE USED TO ARN'S ADVENTURING, BUT WHEN DAWN COMES AND HE HAS NOT RETURNED, A WIDE SEARCH IS INSTITUTED.

THEN ALETA REMEMBERS THE CAVE THAT IS A FAVORITE PLACE TO FISH AND SWIM WITH HIS FRIENDS.

THEIR CLOTHING IS NOT IN THE CAVE, SO THERE COULD BE NO SWIMMING ACCIDENT. THE FIRE IS LAID, FLINT AND STEEL LIE BESIDE IT. THEN VAL SEES THE MARK LEFT IN THE SAND BY THE PROW OF A BOAT.

VAL GOES TO THE ADMINISTRATOR'S OFFICE WHERE LISTS OF ALL THE DAYS EVENTS ARE POSTED. OVER AND OVER HE CHECKS THE LISTS OF EVENTS, SEARCHING FOR SOME CLUE TO ARN'S DISAPPEARANCE.

THREE ITEMS ON THE LIST COME TOGETHER LIKE PIECES OF A PUZZLE. THREE PRISONERS HAVE ESCAPED AND DISAPPEARED; A BOAT STOLEN AND NOT FOUND; THREE CHILDREN MISSING TOO!

VAL COMMANDS GUNDAR HARL TO MAKE READY HIS SHIP.

1253.

2-12-61

THE FATE OF THE CAPTIVES IS DISCUSSED QUITE OPENLY. PRINCE ARN IS TO BE RANSOMED, THE OTHER TWO SOLD TO A SLAVE DEALER.

NEXT WEEK—**A Bid for Freedom**

Our Story: PRINCE VALIANT BELIEVES THAT THE ESCAPE OF THREE PRISONERS, THE THEFT OF A BOAT, AND THE DISAPPEARANCE OF PRINCE ARN ARE ALL RELATED. HE SETS SAIL TO FIND THE BOAT, TAKING THE OWNER ALONG TO IDENTIFY IT.

"YESTERDAY THE WIND WAS FROM THE SOUTH, SIRE. IT IS MY BELIEF THEY WENT NORTH-WARD. THERE WAS NEITHER FOOD NOR WATER IN MY BOAT, SO THEY MUST LAND SOON."

VAL SEARCHES THE NEAREST ISLANDS AND SOON FINDS WHERE THE FUGITIVES OBTAINED WHAT THEY WANTED. HERE THEY LEFT EVIDENCE OF WHAT MANNER OF MEN THEY ARE.

A FEW DAYS LATER, AGAIN OUT OF FOOD AND WATER, THE FUGITIVES COME TO A GREAT WALLED CITY. HERE THEY CAN HIDE IN THE SLUMS AND SELL THEIR SMALL CAPTIVES.

THE BUSY HARBOR IS CROWDED AND, AS THEY SEEK A PLACE TO MOOR THEIR BOAT, ARN SLIPS OVER-BOARD.

IT SEEMS AS IF HOURS PASS WHILE THE LAD PLAYS HIDE AND SEEK AMONG THE BOATS.

HE IS NEAR EXHAUSTION WHEN AT LAST HE FINDS STEPS THAT LEAD UP TO THE QUAY.

1254.

"TO THE SLAVE MARKET. WE MUST SELL THESE TWO AND THEN SEARCH THE CITY FOR THE OTHER. HIS RANSOM WILL BRING US RICHES!"
NEXT WEEK- **Slaves**

2-19-61

Prince Valiant

IN THE DAYS OF KING ARTHUR

WRITTEN AND ILLUSTRATED BY Harold R Foster

Our Story: PRINCE ARN ESCAPES FROM HIS DESPERATE CAPTORS, BUT BEFORE HE CAN SEEK HELP IN THIS STRANGE CITY, HE SEES HIS TWO COMPANIONS BEING LED TO THE SLAVE MARKET.

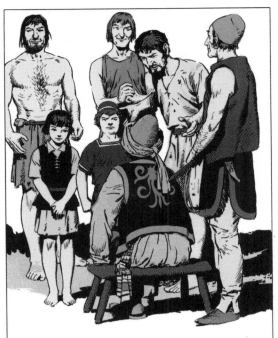

AFTER MUCH HAGGLING A BARGAIN IS MADE WITH THE AUCTIONEER.

"STRIP THEM OF THEIR GARMENTS," ORDERS THE SLAVE MASTER, " THE BUYERS MUST SEE THAT THEIR BODIES ARE WITH-OUT BLEMISH."

DIANE IS A PEASANT, SHE WILL ACCEPT HER FATE AND PATIENTLY MAKE THE BEST OF IT.... SHE WILL SURVIVE. BUT PAUL IS OF NOBLE BIRTH, HE FIGHTS WILDLY, BRAVELY AND PERHAPS FOOLISHLY.

THE SLAVE MASTER LOSES HIS PATIENCE AND WITH A BRUTAL BLOW SENDS THE LAD SPRAWLING.

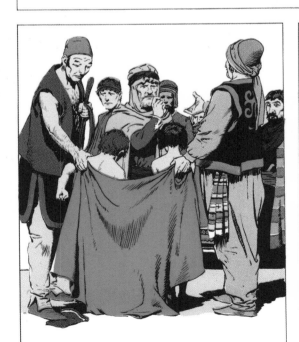

THEY ARE PURCHASED BY A BUYER FROM NORTH AFRICA WHERE THERE IS A GOOD MARKET FOR CHILDREN.

IN DESPAIR ARN WATCHES AS HIS TWO PLAY-MATES ARE LED AWAY WITH OTHER SLAVES TO THE SLAVER'S SHIP.

1255.

THEN HE HASTENS TO THE GOVERNOR'S PALACE TO SEEK AID.

NEXT WEEK- **Over the Garden Wall**

2-26-61

Prince Valiant
IN THE DAYS OF KING ARTHUR

WRITTEN AND ILLUSTRATED BY HAROLD R FOSTER

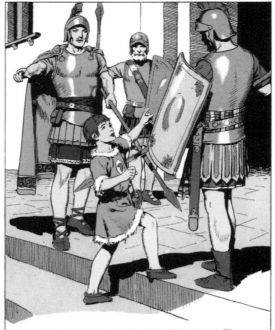

Our Story: ABOARD THE SLAVE SHIP DIANE WIPES THE BLOOD FROM PAUL'S BATTERED FACE. *"BE PATIENT,"* SHE WHISPERS, *"AND AWAIT OUR CHANCE. ARN IS FREE AND MAY YET FIND HELP FOR US."*

PRINCE ARN IS EVEN THEN AT THE GOVERNOR'S PALACE, BUT THE GUARDS DO NOT BELIEVE THIS WET AND DISHEVELED BRAT IS THE ROYAL PRINCE HE CLAIMS TO BE.

BUT HE MUST GET IN TO SEE THE GOVERNOR SOMEHOW. HE WANDERS AROUND THE PALACE SEEKING A WAY IN. SUDDENLY HIS CHANCE COMES.

IN A NARROW ALLEYWAY A COVERED WAGON IS MAKING ITS WAY. WITH A RUNNING LEAP HE GAINS THE WAGON, SCRAMBLES TO THE TOP, AND SPRINGS TO THE GARDEN WALL.

"YOU KNOW THE PENALTY FOR ENTERING THE WOMEN'S COURT?" ASKS A PATRICIAN LADY. *"THAT IS A RISK I TAKE, FOR I MUST SEE THE GOVERNOR,"* ANSWERS ARN BOLDLY.

JUST THEN THE GOVERNOR ENTERS THE GARDEN. HE HAS HAD A GOOD DAY AND ACCEPTED SOME VERY SATISFACTORY BRIBES. *"I DEMAND YOUR AID,"* CRIES ARN, *"FOR I AM PRINCE ARN, SON OF ALETA, QUEEN OF THE MISTY ISLES, AND MY SIRE IS PRINCE VALIANT. SEE, I WEAR THE CRIMSON STALLION CREST OF THE HOUSE OF AGUAR, KING OF THULE!"*

HAL FOSTER

OH, WHAT A PERFECT DAY THIS IS! NOW HE HAS THE HEIR TO A RICH THRONE IN HIS HANDS. HOW CAN HE PROFIT THE MOST FROM THIS?

NEXT WEEK—**Expense Account**

1256.   3-5-61

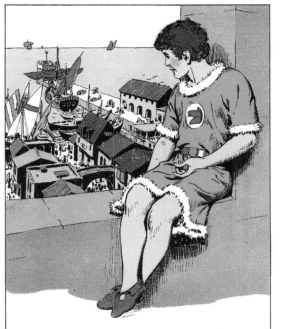

Our Story: IN GUNDAR HARL'S SLEEK SHIP PRINCE VALIANT SCOURS THE SEA IN SEARCH OF HIS SON ARN, SAILING EVER DOWN WIND WHERE THE FUGITIVES' BOAT MUST GO, WHILE THE ANXIOUS DAYS SLIP BY.

PRINCE ARN IS SAFE, BUT A VIRTUAL PRISONER IN A GOVERNOR'S PALACE, AND THE WILY GOVERNOR IS DICTATING A LETTER TO PRINCE VALIANT.

"YOUR SON, PRINCE ARN, HAS BEEN CARRIED OFF BY PIRATES, BUT WE WILL SEND OUR OWN FLEET TO PUNISH THESE PIRATES AND BRING BACK YOUR SON. OF COURSE YOU MUST SHARE OUR GREAT EXPENSE," AND HE NAMES A HUGE SUM.

THE COURIER IS LUCKY. HE DOES NOT HAVE TO SAIL ALL THE WAY TO THE MISTY ISLES, FOR HE MEETS VAL'S SHIP A FEW LEAGUES AWAY AND DELIVERS THE MESSAGE.

ARN IS TORN BETWEEN JOY AND DESPAIR AS, FROM HIS TOWER WINDOW, HE SEES GUNDAR HARL'S SHIP ENTER THE HARBOR, WHILE THE SLAVE SHIP IN WHICH DIANE AND PAUL ARE HELD SPREADS ITS SAILS TO A FAVORABLE WIND AND HEADS FOR AFRICA.

ARN SEES HIS FATHER APPROACH. HE CALLS BUT IS UNHEARD, SO HE PUTS A FLOWER POT IN HIS TUNIC.....

.....AND PROVES TO VAL THAT HIS SON IS ALIVE AND HIS AIM IS STILL GOOD.

THE GOVERNOR IS TREMBLING. HE RECOGNIZES THE LETTER AND THE TUNIC, AND HE SUSPECTS THAT THE UNFRIENDLY PERSON HOLDING THEM IS PRINCE VALIANT.
NEXT WEEK- **Paul's Ordeal**

1257.   3-12-61

Our Story: THE GOVERNOR LOOKS AT THE EVIDENCE OF HIS LITTLE SCHEME TO MAKE A FAIR PROFIT. HAD HE KNOWN PRINCE VALIANT WOULD TURN OUT TO BE SUCH A FRIGHTENING PERSON, HE WOULD NOT HAVE TRIED IT. THEN HE REMEMBERS HE HAS A WHOLE GARRISON AT HIS COMMAND AND BECOMES ARROGANT.

HIS BLUSTER DIES AWAY UNDER THE STEADY GAZE. HE SENDS FOR ARN.

"GREETINGS, SIRE, THANKS FOR COMING, BUT WE MUST HURRY!" CRIES ARN BREATHLESSLY. "PAUL AND DIANE ARE PRISONERS ON THAT SHIP THAT JUST SAILED, BOUND FOR THE SLAVE MARKETS OF AFRICA! AND I KNOW WHERE OUR ABDUCTORS ARE!"

FROM HIS TOWER ROOM ARN HAD SEEN THE THREE FUGITIVES GO IN AND OUT OF A WATERFRONT WINE SHOP. THEY OFFER VERY LITTLE RESISTANCE.

ABOARD THE SLAVE SHIP PAUL AND DIANE, NOW BUT TWO SMALL BITS OF HUMAN MERCHANDISE, AWAIT THEIR FATE, SHE PATIENTLY, HE FIGHTING EVERY MINUTE.

NOT A DAY PASSES THAT HE DOES NOT FEEL THE SLAVE-MASTER'S LASH. HE WILL NOT SURVIVE TO BE A SLAVE!

LEAGUE BY LEAGUE THE DISTANCE BETWEEN THE LUMBERING DHOW AND THE RESCUE SHIP GROWS SMALLER.

NEXT WEEK - **The Swap**

1258.

3-19-61

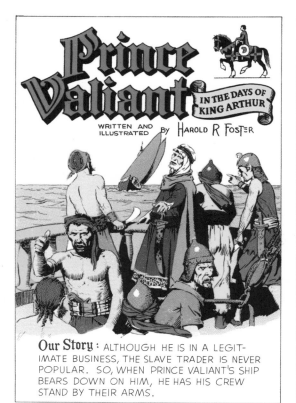

Prince Valiant
IN THE DAYS OF KING ARTHUR
WRITTEN AND ILLUSTRATED BY HAROLD R FOSTER

Our Story: ALTHOUGH HE IS IN A LEGITIMATE BUSINESS, THE SLAVE TRADER IS NEVER POPULAR. SO, WHEN PRINCE VALIANT'S SHIP BEARS DOWN ON HIM, HE HAS HIS CREW STAND BY THEIR ARMS.

THE SWIFTER SHIP COMES UP TO WINDWARD AND TAKES THE WIND FROM THE SLAVE SHIP'S SAILS. GRAPPLES ARE THROWN, AND THE TWO VESSELS ARE LOCKED TOGETHER.

VAL DEMANDS THE TWO CHILDREN, BUT THE SLAVE TRADER, HAVING A STRONGER CREW, REFUSES, DEMANDING A HUGE PRICE.

IT IS THE KIDNAPPERS WHO OFFER THE SOLUTION, FOR THEY HAVE ABDUCTED A ROYAL PRINCE AND FACE A FEARFUL DOOM. IT IS BETTER TO BE SLAVES.

THREE STRONG MEN FOR THE TWO CHILDREN IS A GOOD BARGAIN. THE SLAVER SENDS HIS BRUTAL SLAVE-MASTER TO UNSHACKLE PAUL AND DIANE.

THE EXCHANGE IS MADE AND ALL PROBLEMS ARE SOLVED....... BUT ONE.

PAUL HAS FELT THE CARESS OF THE LASH, AND, BEING AN HONEST LAD, FEELS THAT HE SHOULD PAY FOR THIS ATTENTION.

1259.

SO, WITH A MIGHTY HEAVE, THE SCORE IS EVENED.
NEXT WEEK—Aleta's Burden

3-26-61

Our Story: ALETA, QUEEN OF THE MISTY ISLES, IS AT THE END OF HER STRENGTH. HER NEWBORN SON DEMANDS ATTENTION, PRINCE VALIANT IS AT SEA SEARCHING FOR PRINCE ARN WHO HAS BEEN ABDUCTED, A WAR HAS JUST ENDED.

A THOUSAND PRISONERS OF WAR AND A HUNDRED CAPTURED SHIPS MUST BE PUT TO WORK, AND VICTORY HAS BROUGHT MANY NEW RESPONSIBILITIES.

THEN VAL AND ARN WALK IN AS CALMLY AS IF THERE WERE NOTHING IN THE WIDE WORLD TO WORRY ABOUT!

ALETA'S TIRED EYES GROW BRIGHT WITH ANGER. TIGHT AS A BOWSTRING SHE STANDS BEFORE HER HUSBAND AND BERATES HIM, HER VOICE SHRILL WITH HYSTERIA!

THEN SHE THROWS HERSELF INTO HIS ARMS, SOBBING WILDLY, BEGGING FOR FORGIVENESS. VAL HOLDS HER TENDERLY, MARVELLING AT HOW THIN SHE HAS BECOME AS HE TRIES TO COMFORT HER.

HE PLACES HER GENTLY ON A COUCH AND, AS HE LOOSENS HER HAIR, SHE FALLS ASLEEP.
"IS SHE ILL, KATWIN?" HE ASKS.
"NO, SIRE, ONLY TIRED BEYOND ENDURANCE."

THE LINES OF ANXIETY FADE SLOWLY FROM HER FACE AS VAL WATCHES, FASCINATED. FOR HE HAS JUST MADE A DISCOVERY: HIS WONDROUS QUEEN IS BUT A MORTAL WOMAN AFTER ALL!

NEXT WEEK - **The New Era**

1260.   4-2-61

HAL FOSTER

Prince Valiant
IN THE DAYS OF KING ARTHUR
WRITTEN AND ILLUSTRATED BY HAROLD R FOSTER

Our Story: PRINCE VALIANT RETURNS TO HIS GROWING FAMILY, SO CALM, SO STRONG AND CONFIDENT, A PILLAR OF STRENGTH FOR ALETA TO LEAN UPON. HE LENDS HER THE STAMINA TO FACE THE DIFFICULT ROAD AHEAD.

VICTORY HAS BROUGHT A NEW ERA TO THE MISTY ISLES. THE CAPTURED FLEET MUST BE PUT INTO TRADE; DOCKS AND WAREHOUSES SECURED IN ALEXANDRIA, JAFFA, BEIRUT AND CONSTANTINOPLE. THE DAY OF THE TRAVELING SALESMAN HAS ARRIVED.

ONCE FRIENDLY AMBASSADORS CAME TO THE PEACEFUL KINGDOM; NOW THEY COME WITH GREEDY EYES TO ESTIMATE THE STRENGTH OF THE WALLS, TO WHEEDLE CRAFTILY, TO FAWN FOR FAVORS.

THE SECRET COVE HAS LOST ITS CHARM. SINCE THEIR PERILOUS ADVENTURE, THERE HAS COME A CHANGE. DIANE IS NOW A SHY YOUNG GIRL; PAUL WANTS TO BE PART OF THE EXCITING NEW ORDER, AND ARN YEARNS TO TAKE HIS PLACE BESIDE HIS HERO, PRINCE VALIANT, AND GO ADVENTURING ACROSS THE WORLD.

ANOTHER THING HAS BEEN CHANGED..... OFTEN. A LOUD AND LUSTY PRINCE MUST BE CHRISTENED WITH ENOUGH POMP AND CEREMONY TO IMPRESS THE NEIGHBORS WITH HIS IMPORTANCE.

1261.

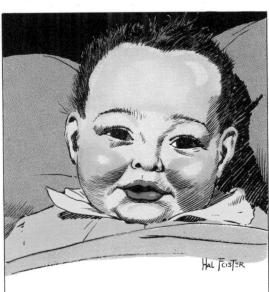

HAL FOSTER

STILL NAMELESS, KNOWING NEITHER LOVE NOR HATE, WITHOUT GREED OR LEARNING, THIS SMALL ENTITY BEGINS HIS HAZARDOUS CLIMB TO A THRONE.

NEXT WEEK- **The Christening**

4-9-61

Prince Valiant
IN THE DAYS OF KING ARTHUR

WRITTEN AND ILLUSTRATED BY Harold R. Foster

Our Story: FROM NEAR AND FAR EMISSARIES ARRIVE IN POMP AND SPLENDOR, BEARING RICH GIFTS FOR THE PRINCE APPARENT TO THE THRONE OF THE MISTY ISLES. NOW THAT THIS KINGDOM PROMISES TO BECOME RICH AND POWERFUL, IT IS DEEMED WISE TO BE GENEROUS.

FINDING A NAME IS NOT EASY. ANCESTORS MUST BE REMEMBERED, THE GODS, EMPERORS AND KINGS, RELATIVES AND FRIENDS. THE LIST GROWS LONG. *"WHY NOT JUST CALL HIM GALAN,"* SUGGESTS ARN, *"IT HAS A GOOD SOUND AND NO ONE WILL FEEL LEFT OUT."*

THE CHRISTENING IS A HUGE SUCCESS. ALETA NEVER LOOKED LOVELIER AND SEVERAL OF HER OLD SUITORS PRESENT HEAVE DOLOROUS SIGHS FOR 'WHAT MIGHT HAVE BEEN'. PRINCE VALIANT BEHAVES WITH THE CONFIDENCE OF LONG PRACTICE (THIS IS HIS FOURTH PERFORMANCE). THE BABY KEEPS QUIET UNTIL THE ARCHBISHOP SAYS 'GALAN' AND SPRINKLES THE WATER, THEN HE YELLS SO LUSTILY THAT THE REST OF THE NAMES ARE LOST IN THE NOISE.

NEXT WEEK- **The Storm**

1262.

HAL FOSTER

4-16-61

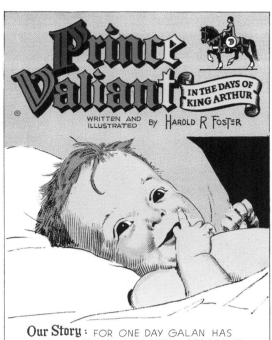

Prince Valiant
IN THE DAYS OF KING ARTHUR

WRITTEN AND ILLUSTRATED By HAROLD R FOSTER

Our Story: FOR ONE DAY GALAN HAS BEEN THE MOST IMPORTANT PERSON IN THE KINGDOM. AMID POMP AND CIRCUMSTANCE HE HAS BEEN CHRISTENED AND DECLARED HEIR TO THE THRONE, AND NOW..... BACK TO THE NURSERY.

THERE TO BE LOVED AND SPOILED UNTIL THAT TIME WHEN HE IS READY FOR DISCIPLINE AND TRAINING LIKE THE OTHER MEMBERS OF ALETA'S NUMEROUS BROOD.

AND NOW PRINCE VALIANT TAKES OVER ARN'S TRAINING PERSONALLY. NO LONGER ARE HIS LESSONS PLAY, BUT SERIOUS BUSINESS, AND HE WORKS HARD TO WIN THAT ONE WORD OF PRAISE THAT HE LONGS FOR FROM HIS SIRE.

ALETA, WATCHING, REMEMBERS WHEN SHE SAID: "SOON ENOUGH HE WILL HAVE THE LOOK OF EAGLES AND WILL RIDE WITH YOU ABOUT MAN'S WORK. UNTIL THEN HE IS MINE TO LOVE AND CARE FOR!" THAT TIME HAS COME.

BY WAYS KNOWN ONLY TO SAILORS A GREAT STORM IS FORECAST, AND ALL THE SHIPS IN THE HARBOR ARE BEING MADE READY FOR IT.

1263.　4-23-61

HAL FOSTER

VAL AND ARN GO TO THE HEADLAND THAT PROTECTS THE HARBOR AND THERE, ON THE HORIZON, ARE GREAT STORM CLOUDS, BLACK AND OMINOUS AND FLASHING FIRE. IN THE DISTANCE A SHIP IS STRAINING TO REACH THE SAFETY OF THE HARBOR.
NEXT WEEK- The Wreck

Prince Valiant

IN THE DAYS OF KING ARTHUR

WRITTEN AND ILLUSTRATED BY HAROLD R FOSTER

Our Story: PRINCE VALIANT AND ARN WATCH, FASCINATED, AS THE GALLANT SHIP CROWDS ON SAIL TO REACH THE SHELTER OF THE HARBOR BEFORE THE ONRUSHING STORM.

BUT THE STORM IS NOT TO BE DENIED AND ROARS DOWN UPON THE SHIP AND WOULD HAVE CAPSIZED IT HAD NOT THE VERY FORCE OF THE WIND RIPPED THE SAILS TO SHREDS. ONE PERIL GIVES WAY TO ANOTHER AS THE VESSEL DRIFTS HELPLESSLY TOWARDS THE ROCKS.

VAL AND ARN WAIT ON THE BEACH. ABOVE THE THUNDER OF WIND AND WAVE THEY CAN HEAR THE CRIES FOR HELP COMING FROM THE CROWDED DECK.

SOON THE BEACH IS STREWN WITH WRECKAGE, AND FATHER AND SON HELP THE LIVING THROUGH THE UNDERTOW. AND THESE ARE ALL TOO FEW!

ONE WHO SEEMS TO BE THEIR LEADER CALLS VAL TO HIS SIDE. "WE ARE PILGRIMS BOUND FOR THE HOLY LAND. WE HAVE BEEN A YEAR ON OUR WAY AND NOW, SO CLOSE TO OUR GOAL, COMES DISASTER. MY FOLLOWERS SEEK REDEMPTION FROM THEIR SINS BY THIS PILGRIMAGE."

1264.   4-30-61

HAL FOSTER

"I SEE BY THE GOLDEN CHAIN YOU WEAR THAT YOU ARE A NOBLE AND OF FAIR WEALTH. WILL YOU AID US TO FULFILL OUR OATH AND COME AT LAST TO THE HOLY CITY AND PEACE?"

NEXT WEEK - **The Pilgrims**

Our Story: A PILGRIM SHIP, BOUND FOR THE HOLY LAND, IS WRECKED AND PRINCE VALIANT AND ARN RISK THEIR LIVES TO RESCUE WHOM THEY CAN. HELP ARRIVES TO GATHER IN WHAT LITTLE THE SULLEN SEA GIVES UP.

THE LEADER, SIR OWEN OF LOTHIAN, PLEADS WITH VAL TO AID THE PILGRIMS REACH THEIR GOAL.

WHEN VAL GOES TO THE PORT AUTHORITY TO SECURE PASSAGE FOR THE PILGRIMS, HE HEARS DISQUIETING NEWS. ALETA'S CAPTAINS ARE UNFAMILIAR WITH THE PEOPLE ALONG THE NEW TRADE ROUTE AND CARGOES ARE HARD TO COME BY.

"I WILL SAIL WITH THE PILGRIMS TO JAFFA; THEN, AS YOUR AMBASSADOR, TRAVEL THE TRADE ROUTE AND PROMOTE BUSINESS FOR OUR SHIPS."
"AND WILL YOU TAKE ARN WITH YOU?", ASKS ALETA.

"HAS THE TIME COME ALREADY?", WONDERS VAL. "YES", ANSWERS ALETA WITH PAIN IN HER HEART.
"HE HAS BECOME A MAN-CHILD NOW AND MUST LEARN MEN'S WAYS. YES, IT IS TIME."

1265.

THE DAY HE HAS DREAMED OF FOR SO LONG HAS COME AT LAST. HE IS TO GO ADVEN-TURING WITH HIS SIRE!
THEN HE SEES HIS MOTHER WAVE GOODBYE AND FOR A WILD MOMENT HE WANTS TO LEAP ASHORE AND RUN TO HER SIDE. BUT HE BLINKS RAPIDLY, SWALLOWS THE LUMP IN HIS THROAT AND WAVES BACK BRAVELY.
NEXT WEEK— The Pilgrims' Goal   5-7-61

Prince Valiant
IN THE DAYS OF KING ARTHUR
WRITTEN AND ILLUSTRATED BY HAROLD R FOSTER

Our Story: PRINCE VALIANT BRINGS HIS SHIP SAFELY INTO THE HARBOR OF JAFFA, AND THE PILGRIMS ARE JOYFUL TO BE SO NEAR THEIR GOAL. BUT IT IS MANY DAYS BEFORE THEY PROCEED.

ONLY WHEN SUFFICIENT TRAVELERS HAVE GATHERED AND GUARDS HIRED CAN THEY TAKE THE PERILOUS WAY THROUGH THE HILLS TO JERUSALEM.

THEY ENTER THE CITY BY THE JAFFA GATE. THIS IS VAL'S THIRD VISIT AND HE IS AWARE OF A GROWING HOSTILITY THE PEOPLE SHOW TO THE PILGRIMS.

TO SOME OF THE PILGRIMS HAS COME HUMILITY BUT TO OTHERS THE HARDSHIPS OF THE LONG JOURNEY HAVE CHANGED FAITH TO FANATICISM, AND TO THESE VAL PLEADS: *"RESPECT THE BELIEFS AND CUSTOMS OF OTHERS THAT FUTURE PILGRIMS BE NOT ENDANGERED."*

HAD THIS ADVICE BEEN HEEDED THERE WOULD HAVE BEEN NO CRUSADES. ARN IS WIDE-EYED WITH WONDER AS HIS FATHER SHOWS HIM THE SACRED PLACES OF THE HOLY CITY.

THEY LEAVE BY THE JERICHO ROAD, DOWN THE VALLEY OF THE KEDRON. ON ONE SIDE THE MOUNT OF OLIVES AND THE GARDEN OF GETHSEMANE, ON THE OTHER THE GRIM CITY WALLS.

1266

EVER DOWNWARD THE ROAD WINDS. WHERE ONCE GARDENS FLOURISHED IS DESERT, AND THE HUGE MOUNDS OF RUBBLE WERE ONCE THE CITY OF JERICHO.
IN THE DISTANCE THE DEAD SEA GLITTERS AND THE HILLS OF THE MOAB SHIMMER IN THE HEAT. PRINCE ARN SWAYS, FAINTING IN THE SADDLE.

NEXT WEEK— **The Slave**

5-14-61

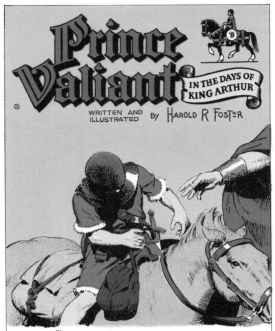

Prince Valiant

IN THE DAYS OF KING ARTHUR

WRITTEN AND ILLUSTRATED BY HAROLD R FOSTER

Our Story: HERE ON THE SHORES OF THE DEAD SEA THE SUN CAN BE AN EVIL THING. ARN SWAYS, FAINTING IN HIS SADDLE AND WOULD HAVE FALLEN HAD NOT PRINCE VALIANT CAUGHT HIM.

HE HAD BEEN SO PROUD OF HIS NEW SWORD, SHIELD, COIF OF CHAIN MAIL AND HELMET THAT HE HAD INSISTED ON WEARING THEM. THE HELMET BURNS VAL'S FINGERS AS HE REMOVES IT.

IT IS BUT A SHORT DISTANCE TO THE RIVER JORDAN AND THERE THEY PUT THE LAD TO SOAK IN THE COOL WATER.

TOWARD EVENING A CARAVAN APPROACHES. A RICH MERCHANT IS TAKING RUGS, INCENSE AND SLAVES TO THE MARKET. THEY SET UP THEIR TENTS IN THE GROVE NEARBY.

PRINCE VALIANT, KNIGHT, NOW SALESMAN, ENTERTAINS THE MERCHANT AND CONVINCES HIM THAT HE SHOULD TRADE THROUGH ALETA'S AGENTS IN JAFFA. DURING THIS TIME VAL BECOMES INTERESTED IN SOME OF THE MERCHANDISE......

....A SLAVE, UNSHACKLED BUT WEARING A SLAVE COLLAR. HE IS KEEPING ACCOUNTS FOR THE MERCHANT AND HIS DARK EYES ARE FILLED WITH DESPAIR.

1267

THE MERCHANT WOULD SELL ANYTHING FOR A PRICE, BUT IT IS NEAR MIDNIGHT WHEN THE HAGGLING ENDS AND THE PRICE IS PAID.

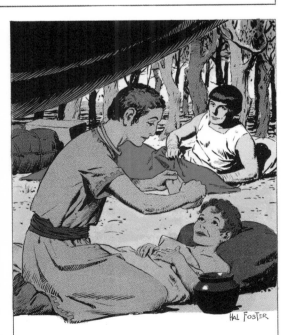

VAL AWAKES LATE. THE NEW SLAVE IS APPLYING A COOL COMPRESS TO ARN'S FOREHEAD.
NEXT WEEK- **Ohmed, the Slave.**

HAL FOSTER

5-21-61

Prince Valiant
IN THE DAYS OF KING ARTHUR
WRITTEN AND ILLUSTRATED BY Harold R Foster

Our Story: PRINCE VALIANT'S FIRST CONCERN IS FOR HIS SON ARN. THE LAD WANTS TO GO ON, BUT OHMED QUIETLY ADVISES A DAY OF REST WHILE HE FASHIONS PROPER DRESS FROM THE TRADE GOODS.

THIS IS THE FIRST SLAVE VAL HAS EVER BOUGHT AND HE IS QUITE PLEASED WITH HIS PURCHASE, FOR OHMED CAN KEEP ACCOUNTS, CONDUCT THE CARAVAN AND SPEAK THE LANGUAGES OF THE COUNTRIES THEY PROPOSE TO TRAVEL THROUGH.

THEY FERRY ACROSS THE JORDAN AND TAKE THE AGE-OLD ROUTE TO GALILEE AND THE CITY OF TIBERIAS.

AND THERE VAL MAKES A SAD DISCOVERY. HE CAN MEET PRINCES AND KINGS ON EQUAL TERMS BUT HE IS NO MATCH FOR THE WILY MERCHANTS HE NOW HAS TO DEAL WITH. HE NEEDS A BUSINESS MANAGER WHO KNOWS THE WORLD OF TRADE.

INTO SYRIA, AND THE DAMASCUS ROAD LEADS THROUGH A FERTILE LAND WITH THE MOUNTAINS OF LEBANON IN THE DISTANCE. BUT VAL IS TROUBLED, HE DOUBTS IF ALETA'S MERCHANT TRADE CAN SURVIVE HIS POOR MANAGEMENT.

DAMASCUS, THE WORLD'S OLDEST OCCUPIED CITY, STANDS GLEAMING IN THE SUNLIGHT, WHILE THE LEGION OF CONQUERORS WHO HAVE RULED HER HAVE BECOME DUST, FORGOTTEN.

IN THE GATEWAY STANDS A HANDSOME YOUNG GREEK. HE IS PENNILESS BECAUSE OF THE DICE, AND WITHOUT EMPLOYMENT BECAUSE THE MONEY HE LOST WAS NOT HIS.

HE SCANS THE INCOMING TRAVELERS WITH A VIEW TO IMPROVING HIS FORTUNE. PRINCE VALIANT HAS THE APPEARANCE OF WEALTH AND INNOCENCE. HE FOLLOWS HIM INTO THE CITY.

NEXT WEEK- **The Business Manager**

1268.   5-28-61

Prince Valiant
IN THE DAYS OF KING ARTHUR
WRITTEN AND ILLUSTRATED BY Harold R Foster

Our Story: AT THE GATES OF DAMASCUS A YOUNG GREEK JOINS PRINCE VALIANT'S CARAVAN AND, FROM ONE OF THE DROVERS, LEARNS ENOUGH TO MAKE SURE THAT HE CAN IMPROVE HIS FORTUNE BY JOINING THE PARTY.

PATIENTLY HE WAITS UNTIL VAL HAS FINISHED THE BUSINESS OF THE DAY. THEN HE RISES, ARRANGES THE FOLDS OF HIS CLOAK, BOWS RESPECTFULLY AND SAYS:

"NOBLE SIR, BY YOUR BEARING IT IS PLAIN THAT YOU ARE MORE QUALIFIED TO DEAL WITH HIGH OFFICIALS THAN SLY MERCHANTS. NOW, I, SIR, AM SHREWD, LESS THAN HONEST, THOROUGHLY UNTRUSTWORTHY AND CAN GUIDE YOU AROUND THE PITFALLS OF BUSINESS......FOR A PRICE OF COURSE!"

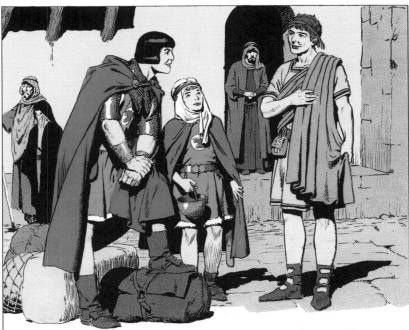

VAL LAUGHS, "I AM IN NEED OF THE TALENTS YOU BOAST OF. COME WITH US TO THE MARKET PLACE AND THERE PIT YOUR SKILLS AGAINST THE WILY TRADERS. IF YOU BARGAIN WELL, YOU MAY NAME YOUR PRICE."

THIS IS STRICTLY TRADE, MONEY IS SELDOM USED, AND THE GOODS FROM THE WEST ARE EXCHANGED FOR THOSE OF THE EAST. AND VAL, WHO IS THE 'TAKE IT OR LEAVE IT' KIND OF BARGAINER, IS AMAZED AT THE SKILL OF HIS NEW BUSINESS MANAGER.

AND WHEN IT COMES TO DRAWING UP CONTRACTS FOR THE SHIPPERS WHO WILL USE THE SHIPS OF THE MISTY ISLES, HE IS A JEWEL BEYOND PRICE.

AT EVENING TWO YOUNG MEN MEET TO RECORD THE BUSINESS OF THE DAY. OHMED, QUIET, STUDIOUS; AND NICILOS, THE GREEK, CLEVER AND GAY. PERHAPS IT IS BECAUSE OF THE GREAT DIFFERENCE IN THEIR NATURES THAT THEIR LIFELONG FRIENDSHIP IS BORN. BUT, OH! HOW SHORT THAT 'LIFELONG' IS TO BE!

NEXT WEEK- The Outcast

HAL FOSTER

1269.   6-4-61

Our Story : PRINCE VALIANT LEADS HIS CARA-
VAN OUT OF DAMASCUS. HIS TWO SERVANTS,
OHMED AND NICILOS, HANDLE THE COMPLI-
CATED DETAILS OF ORGANIZING THE TRAIN
WITH THE EASE OF LONG EXPERIENCE. VAL
BELIEVES THAT NOW HIS VENTURE INTO BUSI-
NESS WILL BE SUCCESSFUL.

THE ROAD TO ALEPPO WINDS THROUGH THE 'HOLLOW LAND' OF SYRIA. THE CRUMBLING
RUINS OF FORTRESS AND TEMPLE SHOW THE MARK OF MANY CONQUERORS; ROMAN AND
GREEK, EGYPTIAN, ASSYRIAN AND PERSIAN STAND ON THE RUBBLE OF YET MORE ANCIENT
INVADERS.

FAR, FAR TO THE EAST A YOUNG GIRL, WHO HAS DEFIED
THE LAWS OF HER TRIBE, STANDS BEFORE THE ELDERS
AND RECEIVES THE DEATH SENTENCE: "WALK WESTWARD!"

SO SHE LEAVES THE BLACK TENTS OF HER PEOPLE, WHO ARE BOUND
BY LAW TO KILL HER SHOULD SHE FACE IN ANY OTHER DIRECTION.
AHEAD THE BARREN STEPPES STRETCH, A WATERLESS WASTE WHERE
A BITTER WIND EVER BLOWS.

AT DAY'S END SHE MEETS A PARTY OF HER
OWN TRIBE RETURNING FROM A RAID.
THEY HAVE NOT HEARD OF HER DOOM!
"I WAS ROUNDING UP STRAYS WHEN MY
HORSE BROKE ITS LEG", SHE LIES.
1270.

THEY GIVE HER A MOUNT, AND WHEN DARK-
NESS COMES SHE SLIPS AWAY AND DISAPPEARS
INTO THE NIGHT.
6-11-61

ALL ASIA LIES BETWEEN THIS FUGITIVE GIRL
AND THE SLOW-MOVING CARAVAN, BUT EACH
DAY THE DISTANCE WILL GROW LESS.

NEXT WEEK - East and West

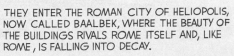
THEY ENTER THE ROMAN CITY OF HELIOPOLIS, NOW CALLED BAALBEK, WHERE THE BEAUTY OF THE BUILDINGS RIVALS ROME ITSELF AND, LIKE ROME, IS FALLING INTO DECAY.

THE ACROPOLIS AT BAALBEK

GATEWAY TO THE TEMPLE OF THE SUN

SO FAR THE JOURNEY HAS BEEN MILDLY SUCCESSFUL AND A LETTER IS SENT TO ALETA IN THE MISTY ISLES, SO THEIR STORE OF TRADE GOODS MAY BE REPLENISHED FOR THE LONG TRIP TO BAGDAD.

Prince Valiant IN THE DAYS OF KING ARTHUR
WRITTEN AND ILLUSTRATED BY HAROLD R FOSTER

Our Story: TO TRAVEL THE HOLY LAND AND SEE THE PLACES MADE FAMILIAR IN THE BIBLE STORY FILLS PRINCE ARN WITH WIDE-EYED WONDER. PRINCE VALIANT IS PROUD THAT HIS SON IS SO WELL INFORMED.

WHEN THE LISTS ARE CHECKED IT IS FOUND THAT SOME GOODS ARE UNACCOUNTED FOR. IT IS A MYSTERY FOR WHICH NO ONE CAN BE BLAMED. NICILOS, THOUGH, IS ALL ARRAYED IN A NEW TUNIC.

A THOUSAND MILES AWAY A YOUNG GIRL, OUTCAST AND CONDEMNED TO DEATH BY HER TRIBE, ESCAPES ACROSS THE BARREN STEPPES. HUNGER HAS BROUGHT DEATH VERY NEAR WHEN SHE ENCOUNTERS A CARAVAN.

THEY HAVE STRAYED FROM THE TRADE ROUTE AND ARE WITHOUT WATER. THE GIRL GUIDES THEM TO A WATERHOLE AND THEN BACK TO THE TRAIL.

SHE IS ALLOWED TO TRAVEL WITH THE CARAVAN, ONE UNPROTECTED GIRL ALONE AMONG ALL THESE FIERCE AND LONELY MEN.

HAL FOSTER

BACK IN THE MISTY ISLES ALETA RECEIVES A LETTER FROM VAL. IT IS A VERY UNROMANTIC LIST OF TRADE GOODS BUT IT ENDS WITH A FEW WORDS THAT LEAVE HER DREAMY AND MISTY-EYED.
NEXT WEEK- **Aleppo**

1271.

6-18-61

Prince Valiant
IN THE DAYS OF KING ARTHUR
WRITTEN AND ILLUSTRATED BY HAROLD R FOSTER

GATE OF THE CITADEL, ALEPPO

Our Story: PRINCE VALIANT LEADS HIS CARAVAN INTO ALEPPO TO END THE FIRST LEG OF THE JOURNEY. HERE A BAGGAGE TRAIN WILL COME UP FROM ANTIOCH BEARING TRADE GOODS FOR THE TRIP TO BAGDAD AND CARRY BACK TO THE MISTY ISLES THE FRUITS OF HIS LABORS SO FAR.

AFTER A FEW DAYS OF WHAT SEEMS HOPELESS CONFUSION VAL'S CARAVAN IS AT LAST READY TO START ITS LONG JOURNEY TO THE EAST.

AND FAR TO THE EAST BUT RIDING WESTWARD IS THE GIRL WHO IS ESCAPING THE DEATH SENTENCE OF HER TRIBE. THE TRADERS SHE IS TRAVELING WITH ENVY HER HORSEMANSHIP.

FOR SHE COMES FROM A TRIBE OF HORSEMEN, BORN TO THE SADDLE, WHO COUNT THEIR WEALTH IN HORSES. HER SKILL MAKES HER A VALUABLE ASSET AND SHE RECEIVES THE PROTECTION OF THE CARAVAN MASTER.

TO THIS WILD DESERT GIRL THE HUGE WALLED TOWNS OF SAMARKAND AND BOKHARA FILL HER WITH WONDER AND FEAR. THE OXUS RIVER IS CROSSED, PERSIA AND THE LONG JOURNEY'S END IS AHEAD.

ON THE SAME DAY VAL SAFELY FERRIES HIS TRAIN ACROSS THE EUPHRATES. HE WILL REACH BAGDAD BY WAY OF THE GOLDEN SICKLE, THAT FERTILE STRIP THAT LIES BETWEEN THE MOUNTAINS AND THE DESERT AND STRETCHES ALL THE WAY FROM SYRIA.

1272.

HAL FOSTER

ONE EVENING AFTER THE TENTS ARE SET UP ARN CLIMBS UP THE MOUNTAINSIDE TO EXPLORE AN ANCIENT RUIN.

NEXT WEEK- **The Tower of Fear**

6-25-61

Prince Valiant
IN THE DAYS OF KING ARTHUR

WRITTEN AND ILLUSTRATED BY Harold R. Foster

Our Story: ONE EVENING PRINCE ARN CLIMBS A HILLSIDE TO EXPLORE AN ANCIENT RUIN. HE WANDERS THROUGH HALLS AND CORRIDORS ALL CHOKED WITH FALLEN MASONRY.

HE COMES TO THE REAR OF THE BUILDING AND THERE CREEPING DOWN THE HILLSIDE IS A BAND OF WILD-LOOKING MOUNTAIN MEN, ARMED AND FURTIVE.

ARN SCRAMBLES TO ESCAPE AND WARN HIS FATHER OF THE LURKING DANGER BUT LOSES HIS WAY......

......AND FINDS HIMSELF IN A CIRCULAR ROOM WITH BUT ONE DOOR. IT IS A TOWER KEEP, AND A FLIGHT OF STEPS LEADS TO THE CRUMBLING TOP.

FROM HIS LOFTY PERCH ARN CAN SEE THE TENTS OF THE CARAVAN AND THE SMOKE RISING FROM THE COOKING FIRES. THEN HE LOOKS AT THE MEN BELOW, AND FROM THEIR GESTURES HE CAN GUESS THAT THEY ARE AWAITING DARKNESS TO ATTACK.

AN ARROW MIGHT ALERT THE CAMP TO THE LURKING DANGER BUT THE DISTANCE IS TOO GREAT. BUT IS IT? AN IDEA IS BORN. QUICKLY HE DRAWS BLOOD AND MARKS AN ARROW.

THEN, WITH ALL THE STRENGTH OF HIS YOUNG BODY HE DRAWS THE BOW TO ITS UTMOST AND SENDS THE BLOODIED MESSENGER TOWARD THE TENTS.

1273.

HAL FOSTER

ANOTHER CARAVAN, THIS ONE FROM THE FAR EAST, COMES TO REST BENEATH THE WALLS OF MERV. BUT FOR A LONELY, HOMESICK GIRL THERE WILL BE NO PEACE.
NEXT WEEK- **The 'Ham'**

7-2-61

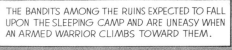

Prince Valiant

IN THE DAYS OF KING ARTHUR

WRITTEN AND ILLUSTRATED BY HAROLD R. FOSTER

Our Story: PRINCE VALIANT RECOGNIZES THE ARROW AS ONE OF ARN'S. *"IT WAS SHOT FROM THAT RUINED TOWER ON THE HILL,"* SAYS NICILOS, *"THE BLOOD UPON IT MUST MEAN DANGER."*

THE BANDITS AMONG THE RUINS EXPECTED TO FALL UPON THE SLEEPING CAMP AND ARE UNEASY WHEN AN ARMED WARRIOR CLIMBS TOWARD THEM.

AS VAL ENTERS THE NARROW DOORWAY HE HEARS HIS SON'S VOICE, *"RAISE YOUR SHIELD, SIRE, AND TURN TO YOUR LEFT."* A WHISTLING ARROW REMOVES THE DANGER TO HIS RIGHT.

BEHIND HIS SHIELD AND THE FLASHING CIRCLE OF THE 'SINGING SWORD' VAL WALKS SLOWLY FORWARD LIKE A REAPER IN A FIELD OF GRAIN. ARROWS WHISTLE AND THUD AMONG HIS ADVERSARIES SO HE KNOWS ARN IS ACTIVE.

LIKE CHAFF BEFORE A WIND THE ILL-ARMED BANDITS MELT AWAY, AND IN THE SILENCE ARN SPEAKS: *"GOOD EVENING, SIRE,"* HE SAYS WITH ELABORATE CALM. *"SHALL WE GO DOWN TO SUPPER?"* *"YES, YOU HAM,"* ANSWERS HIS FATHER.

FAR FROM HER NATIVE DESERT, ALONE AND HOMESICK, A YOUNG GIRL TENDS HER HORSE. HERE IN THIS LAND WOMEN ARE TREATED AS INFERIORS AND WEAR VEILS.

THOSE WHO DO NOT WEAR THE VEIL ARE HELD TO BE SERVANTS OR SLAVES. HOW IS THIS TALL CARAVAN GUARD TO KNOW.......

......THAT HE HAS VIOLATED ONE OF THE STERN LAWS OF A DISTANT TRIBE?

NEXT WEEK - **Escape**

1274.

7-9-61

Prince Valiant
IN THE DAYS OF KING ARTHUR

WRITTEN AND ILLUSTRATED BY Harold R Foster

Our Story: IN A CARAVANSARY OUTSIDE THE CITY OF MERV, THE DESERT GIRL SHEATHES HER NIMBLE KNIFE. SHE HAS DEFENDED HER HONOR ACCORDING TO THE LAWS OF HER TRIBE. BUT WHAT OF THE LAWS OF THIS STRANGE LAND?

SHE GATHERS TOGETHER ALL THE POSSESSIONS OF HER ASSAILANT; THESE ARE HERS BY RIGHT OF CONQUEST. THE DROVERS STAND BACK BEFORE THE THREAT OF THAT GLEAMING SCIMITAR.

SKIRTING THE CITY WALL, SHE RIDES WEST-WARD. OUT ON THE DESERT, ALONE, FREE AND INDEPENDENT, SHE IS HAPPY FOR A WHILE.

WHERE THE SNOWY PEAKS OF THE KOPET DAGH TOWER OVER THE BURNING DESERT SHE OVERTAKES A CARAVAN. IN EXCHANGE FOR HER SKILL IN TENDING THE ANIMALS, SHE IS GIVEN HER KEEP.

AND ONCE AGAIN SHE FEELS THE CONTEMPT THE MEN HAVE FOR AN UNVEILED WOMAN. HER SUPERIOR SKILL AND HORSEMANSHIP ONLY ADD ENVY TO THAT CONTEMPT, AND IN HER PROUD, INDEPENDENT HEART A GREAT ANGER IS GROWING.

BUT IN THAT OTHER CARAVAN COMING FROM THE WEST THERE IS CONTENT, FOR VAL HAS SEEN HIS SON MEET THE CHALLENGE OF DANGER WITH COURAGE AND WIT.

THE ROAD LEADS BY WAY OF GARDENS AND ORCHARDS, ACROSS BARREN WASTELANDS AND THROUGH AWFUL CHASMS, AND EACH DAY BRINGS ARN A NEW WONDER.

THE TIGRIS RIVER AT LAST LEADS THEM TO THAT CITY OF ROMANCE, BAGDAD, AND WEARY MONTHS OF TRAVEL ARE ENDED.

NEXT WEEK— **The Hour of Worship**

1275.   7-16-61

Prince Valiant
IN THE DAYS OF KING ARTHUR
WRITTEN AND ILLUSTRATED BY HAROLD R FOSTER

Our Story: BAGDAD AT LAST! TO PRINCE VALIANT IT MEANS JOURNEY'S END; FROM HERE ALL ROADS LEAD HOMEWARD. TO ARN, A CITY OF WONDER. OHMED, THE SLAVE, IS BUT A FEW MILES FROM HIS HOME. BUT TO NICILOS IT HOLDS A PROMISE OF FROLIC, OF WINE AND GAMING.

IN A CARAVANSARY THE HORSES ARE QUARTERED, GOODS PREPARED FOR TRADING IN THE MARKET PLACE, AND ONE AND ALL LOOK FORWARD TO THE PLEASURES OF THE CITY.

OUT OF THE PERILOUS MOUNTAINS WINDS A WEARY CARAVAN AND FAR IN THE REAR IS A LONELY RIDER, HER HEART FILLED WITH BITTERNESS.

WHEN SHE COMES INTO CAMP IT IS THE HOUR OF PRAYER. ALREADY THE ARABS ARE KNEELING FACING TOWARD MECCA, WHERE STANDS THE BLACK STONE CALLED THE KAABA.

A MAGI HAS SET THE ETERNAL FLAME UPON ITS ALTAR AND THE PERSIANS BOW TO ZOROASTER, LORD OF THE SUN. THEN THE OUTCAST FROM THE BARREN STEPPES BRINGS AN OFFERING TO HER STRANGE GOD, WHOSE SYMBOL IS WATER, GIVER OF LIFE AND FERTILITY.

"OUT WITH YOUR PROFANE GODS!" ROARS THE MAGI. ALL THE PENT-UP ANGER IN HER SOUL BURSTS INTO FLAME AS SHE SPRINGS TO HER FEET.

"SEE," SHE SHRIEKS, "MY GODS ARE STRONGER THAN YOURS." AND THE FLAME THEY HAVE SO CAREFULLY NURTURED ALL THESE WEARY MONTHS IS BUT A PUFF OF STEAM.

1276.

BEFORE SURPRISE CAN TURN INTO ACTION SHE HAS LEAPED TO THE SADDLE AND IS CLATTERING OFF INTO THE TWILIGHT.

NEXT WEEK — **The Road to Bagdad**

7-23-61

Prince Valiant
IN THE DAYS OF KING ARTHUR
WRITTEN AND ILLUSTRATED BY HAROLD R FOSTER

Our Story: NOW THRICE OUTLAWED, THE FUGITIVE ESCAPES INTO THE FOOTHILLS. FOR THE FIRST TIME IN THE LONG LONELY MONTHS SINCE HER BANISHMENT SHE FEELS HAPPINESS.

UNLIKE THE BITTER STEPPES OF HER HOMELAND, HERE ARE WATER, TREES; GAME IS PLENTIFUL AND SHE IS FREE, FREE!

SHE DISTRUSTS CITIES, SO TEHERAN IS CIRCLED FAR OUT IN THE DESERT. BUT AS IF DIRECTED BY THE HAND OF FATE SHE RIDES EVER WESTWARD.

PRINCE VALIANT'S LONG JOURNEY IS CROWNED WITH SUCCESS WHEN THE GUILD OF MERCHANTS AGREES TO USE QUEEN ALETA'S FLEET OF SHIPS TO CARRY THEIR TRADE FROM EAST TO WEST.

WHILE ARN, WIDE-EYED WITH WONDER, WANDERS THROUGH THE BAZAAR. THE SIGHTS AND SOUNDS, THE SMELLS AND COLOR OF BAGDAD WILL LIVE WITH HIM FOREVER.

ONLY OHMED IS UNHAPPY, FOR IT IS QUITE EVIDENT THAT HIS GOOD FRIEND NICILOS HAS BEEN PILFERING FROM THEIR MASTER.

NOT FAR AWAY IS THE VILLAGE THAT WAS ONCE HIS HOME AND HE RECALLS THAT AWFUL DAY THE DESERT MEN MADE THE RAID. TEN YEARS HAVE PASSED, TEN YEARS OF SLAVERY.

NEXT WEEK- **The Return Home**

1277.

7-30-61

Prince Valiant
IN THE DAYS OF KING ARTHUR
WRITTEN AND ILLUSTRATED BY HAROLD R FOSTER

Our Story: WHEN THE DAY'S WORK IS DONE, OHMED THE SLAVE, COMES TO PRINCE VALIANT AND SAYS: "MASTER, I WOULD VISIT MY HOME ONCE AGAIN, IT IS NOT FAR FROM HERE."

"TEN YEARS AGO THE WILD DESERT MEN CAME DOWN ON OUR VILLAGE WITH FIRE AND SWORD. I WAS CARRIED OFF TO SLAVERY AND KNOW NOT IF MY PARENTS STILL LIVE."

VAL HAS HEARD OF SEVERAL WONDERS THAT LIE OUT IN THE DESERT, SO HE AND ARN RIDE WITH OHMED. THE FIRST OF THESE WONDERS IS CTESIPHON.

THEN THEY CROSS A RIVER IN A GUFA AND VAL SAYS: "IT IS NOT RIGHT THAT YOU AT LAST REACH YOUR HOME A SLAVE. I SET YOU FREE." AND HE ORDERS THAT THE SLAVE COLLAR BE STRUCK FROM HIS NECK.

FATHER AND SON COME TO FABULOUS BABYLON AND WANDER AMID THE WRECKAGE THAT TIME AND WAR HAVE MADE OF THE WONDER CITY OF THE ANCIENT WORLD.....

...WHILE OHMED STANDS IN TEARS AMID THE RUIN OF HIS HOME. SUCH WAS THE FEROCITY OF THE RAID THAT NO ONE WAS LEFT TO KEEP THE DESERT FROM RECLAIMING ITS OWN.

FROM A HILLTOP AN OUTCAST LOOKS ACROSS MARSH AND DESERT TO WHERE BAGDAD GLIMMERS IN THE DISTANCE AMID ITS FIELDS AND GARDENS.
MUCH AS SHE HATES AND FEARS THE TEEMING CITIES SHE MUST SELL SOME OF HER POSSESSIONS TO SURVIVE.

NEXT WEEK- The Fateful Meeting

1278.

8-6-61

HAL FOSTER

Prince Valiant
IN THE DAYS OF KING ARTHUR
WRITTEN AND ILLUSTRATED BY HAROLD R FOSTER

Our Story : THREE HORSEMEN RIDE INTO BAGDAD; OHMED, HOMELESS, BUT NO LONGER A SLAVE; PRINCE ARN, FAIRLY BURSTING WITH EXCITEMENT FOR HE HAS SEEN THE RUINS OF BABYLON; AND PRINCE VALIANT, EAGER TO BEGIN THE LONG JOURNEY HOME.

THROUGH ANOTHER GATE RIDES A FIERCE-EYED GIRL TO BARGAIN FOR THE BARE NECESSITIES OF LIFE.

SHE FINDS THE MARKET PLACE AND SETS BEFORE HER THE EXTRA SADDLE AND AWAITS A BUYER. VAL COMES BY AND HIS EYE IS CAUGHT BY THE FINE CONDITION OF HER TWO HORSES.

HORSES HE FINDS CAN BE TRADED ONLY, THEY ARE FAR TOO PRECIOUS TO BE SOLD FOR MONEY. HE SMILES AT HER STRUGGLE WITH THE LANGUAGE AND HER EYES OPEN WIDE WITH PLEASURE. IT IS THE FIRST SMILE SHE HAS SHARED IN ALL THESE LONELY MONTHS!

VAL BUYS THE SADDLE AND AT DAY'S END SHE BRINGS IT TO THE CARAVANSARY.

1279.

VAL STILL WANTS TO DICKER FOR HER FINE HORSES, SO HE INVITES HER TO SHARE THEIR EVENING MEAL. NICILOS AND OHMED ARE INDIGNANT AND GO TO EAT WITH THE DROVERS.

SHE LIES LONG AWAKE THAT NIGHT. NOT SINCE HER BANISHMENT HAS SHE MET A MAN WHO TREATED HER AS A HUMAN BEING. AND SUCH A MAN! SHE COULD FOLLOW HIM TO THE END OF THE EARTH!
NEXT WEEK- Rivals

8-13-61

Our Story: IT SEEMS NATURAL THAT A YOUNG BOY AND A PRIMITIVE GIRL SHOULD UNDERSTAND EACH OTHER. AFTER ALL THESE BITTER, LONELY MONTHS IT IS A RELIEF TO TALK AND, IN HER HALTING SPEECH, SHE TELLS HER STORY TO ARN.

"FATHER, THE GIRL'S NAME IS TALOON AND SHE COMES FROM A TRIBE OF HORSEMEN AND SHE CLAIMS SHE CAN PUT OUR POOR BAGGAGE ANIMALS IN AS FINE CONDITION AS HER OWN SPLENDID MOUNTS."

THE DROVERS ARE SULLEN, THEY ARE PROUD OF THEIR OWN RIDING HORSES BUT TREAT THE BAGGAGE ANIMALS AS LOWLY DRUDGES TO BE WORKED TO THE END.

TALOON GIVES HER INSTRUCTIONS THROUGH PRINCE ARN AND THEY DARE NOT DISOBEY. SOON THE GRUMBLING TURNS TO PRIDE AS THEY SEE THE IMPROVEMENT IN THEIR CHARGES.

VAL IS GRATEFUL FOR TALOON; WITH HER HELP HIS RETURN TO ALETA AND HIS CHILDREN WILL BE SWIFT. OHMED, TOO, HAS DREAMS AND HIS DARK EYES FOLLOW THE PROUD, SELF-SUFFICIENT GIRL IN ADORATION.

NOW THAT HE IS FREE HE CAN TAKE A WIFE HE CAN RETURN TO HIS RUINED VILLAGE AND REBUILD HIS HOME.

AND THERE HE AND TALOON WOULD RAISE AND TRAIN HORSES. WHAT A PARADISE THAT WOULD BE FOR AN EX-SLAVE!

1280.

HAL FOSTER

BUT IS HIS DREAM TO BE NO MORE THAN A PUFF OF SMOKE? WILL SHE EVER LOOK AT HIM AS LONG AS PRINCE VALIANT IS NEAR?

NEXT WEEK- **Jealousy**

8-20-61

Our Story: NICILOS, PRINCE VALIANT'S SHREWD BUSINESS MANAGER, RETURNS FROM THE CITY, HURRIEDLY. HE HAD WON AT THE GAMING TABLE, BUT HIS METHODS WERE QUESTIONED AND HE DARE NOT GO BACK.

HE MUST FIND SOME AMUSEMENT CLOSER AT HAND. THEN HIS EYES FALL UPON TALOON. WHY HAD HE NOT NOTICED HER SAVAGE BEAUTY BEFORE?

HE REGARDS WOMEN AS BRIGHTLY COLORED PLAYTHINGS FOR HIS ENTERTAINMENT. BUT THIS ONE CANNOT UNDERSTAND HIS WIT AND CLEVER SAYINGS. INSTEAD SHE READS HIS INTENTIONS AND HER EYES BLAZE IN ANGER.

TO NICILOS THIS REBUFF IS A CHALLENGE; HE DESIRES MOST WHAT IS DENIED HIM. WHAT HAD BEGUN AS A FLIRTATION NOW BECOMES A BURNING DESIRE. THAT HIS FRIEND OHMED CONFESSES HIS LOVE FOR THE GIRL MAKES NOT AN OUNCE OF DIFFERENCE, FOR HIS CODE IS: 'GET WHAT YOU WANT!'

VAL, EVER-COURTEOUS AND KIND, IS SO PREOCCUPIED WITH THOUGHTS OF RETURNING TO HIS BELOVED ALETA THAT HE DOES NOT NOTICE ......

....THAT TALOON HAS GIVEN HIM HER HEART AND WILL FOLLOW HIM AS LONG AS LIFE LASTS, AS HIS SLAVE IF NEED BE.

AND OHMED, AFTER TEN YEARS OF SLAVERY, IS FREE TO TAKE A WIFE. TALOON IS HIS DREAM OF PARADISE.

BUT NICILOS ALSO DESIRES HER AND WILL USE ALL HIS TRICKS, FAIR OR FOUL, TO GET HIS ENDS.

HOW THE FATES MUST HAVE LAUGHED AS THEY WOVE THE THREADS OF FOUR LIVES INTO THIS TRAGIC MESS. FOR NICILOS IS SHARPENING A DEADLY WEAPON, JEALOUSY!

"SEE HOW OFTEN TALOON VISITS THE TENT OF PRINCE VALIANT! WOULD I WERE A HANDSOME PRINCE SO I COULD COMMAND THE FAVORS OF PRETTY GIRLS."

1281.

OHMED KNOWS HIS MASTER TO BE AN HONORABLE MAN, BUT THE SEEDS OF JEALOUSY HAVE BEEN SOWN AND HATRED BEGINS TO BURN IN HIS HEART LIKE A SMALL FLAME.

NEXT WEEK- **The Final Treachery**

8-27-61

Prince Valiant
IN THE DAYS OF KING ARTHUR
WRITTEN AND ILLUSTRATED BY HAROLD R. FOSTER

Our Story: IN THE BEGINNING NICILOS ONLY WANTED TO AMUSE HIMSELF WITH TALOON, BUT NOW A BURNING DESIRE FOR HER HAS BEREFT HIM OF ALL REASON.

SHE WILL NEVER NOTICE HIM AS LONG AS MATTERS STAND AS THEY ARE. TO BRING ABOUT A CHANGE, NO MATTER WHAT, HE NEVER FAILS TO FAN THE FLAME OF OHMED'S JEALOUSY.

PRINCE VALIANT IS OFTEN WITH HER, FOR HE IS ANXIOUS TO HAVE THE HORSES IN CONDITION FOR A SWIFT JOURNEY HOME. HE IS INNOCENT OF THE EMOTIONS THAT ARE BUILDING UP SO TRAGICALLY AROUND HIM.

THE EVENING MEAL OF LAMB AND RICE, EATEN WITH THE FINGERS, USED TO BE A MERRY AFFAIR. NOW, IN SILENCE, OHMED RISES AND WALKS AWAY, HIS FACE WHITE WITH PAIN, FOR HE CANNOT BEAR TO SEE THE LOOK OF ADORATION IN TALOON'S EYES AS SHE LOOKS AT VAL.

NICILOS ENTERS THEIR TENT, AND THERE IS OHMED SHARPENING HIS DAGGER!

"SO!" HE SNEERS, "THE SLAVE HAS AT LAST BECOME A MAN. MAY YOUR COURAGE HOLD UNTIL YOU HAVE DEFENDED THE WOMAN YOU LOVE. MAY ALL THE GODS LEND STRENGTH TO YOUR ARM!"

1282.

THIS NIGHT, ONE, OR PERHAPS TWO OF HIS RIVALS WILL BE REMOVED, HIS BEST FRIEND OR A KINDLY MASTER. HE IS SICK WITH REMORSE AT HIS OWN TREACHERY. BUT HE DOES NOTHING.
NEXT WEEK - The Fateful Night

9-3-61

Prince Valiant
IN THE DAYS OF KING ARTHUR
WRITTEN AND ILLUSTRATED BY HAROLD R FOSTER

Our Story: OHMED TAKES HIS SHARPENED KNIFE OUT INTO THE NIGHT AND WALKS TOWARD PRINCE VALIANT'S TENT. OH, HOW CLEVER IS THE GLIB TONGUE OF NICILOS! IT HAS TURNED THIS GENTLE YOUTH INTO A KILLER.

VAL AND ARN ARE PREPARING TO RETIRE WHEN HE ENTERS. HE WALKS BEHIND THE FRIEND WHO HAS FREED HIM FROM SLAVERY AND DRAWS HIS KNIFE.

AT ARN'S WARNING SHOUT VAL SWINGS ASIDE, BUT THE KNIFE IS SWIFTER AND PAIN COMES LIKE A SEARING FLAME.

BEFORE ARN CAN REACH HIS SWORD TALOON BURSTS INTO THE TENT. A GLANCE SHOWS HER THE STAINED KNIFE IN OHMED'S HAND AND ON THE GROUND THE MAN SHE SO ARDENTLY BUT HOPELESSLY LOVES.

HIS RAGE HAS SPENT ITSELF. HE STANDS AS ONE IN A DREAM. LOOKING INTO THE GIRL'S TRAGIC FACE, HE CAN CLEARLY SEE THAT HIS MAD DEED WILL BREAK HER HEART AND THAT HIS DREAMS OF A PARADISE ON EARTH ARE AT AN END. MOTIONLESS HE AWAITS HER THRUST.

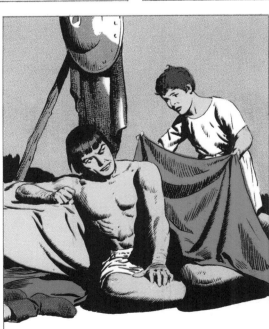

ARN KNEELS BESIDE HIS FATHER AND EXAMINES THE WOUND. "IS IT BAD, SON?" ASKS VAL. "AWFUL, SIRE, WE MUST HAVE HELP."

1283.

HAL FOSTER

NICILOS PEERS FROM HIS TENT. HIS TREACHERY HAS REMOVED ALL RIVALS, BUT HOOFBEATS FADING INTO THE NIGHT INDICATE THE PRIZE IS GONE.

NEXT WEEK—**A Persian Garden**

9-10-61

Our Story: FROM HIS TENT NICILOS WATCHES THE AWFUL RESULTS OF HIS SCHEMING. A MAGI TAKES THE BODY OF POOR OHMED TO THE TEMPLE OF ZOROASTER FOR FUNERAL SERVICES.....

.....WHILE A PALANQUIN BEARS THE WOUNDED PRINCE VALIANT TO THE HOME OF A WEALTHY MERCHANT.

THE WAY LEADS THROUGH NOISOME ALLEYS, CROWDED AND STIFLING.

BUT A DOORWAY OPENS INTO A COURTYARD WHERE FOUNTAINS PLAY AND FLOWERS BLOOM. THEIR HOST WELCOMES THEM AND SENDS FOR HIS OWN PHYSICIAN TO HEAL VAL'S WOUND.

"A VERY CLUMSY PIECE OF WORK," MUTTERS THE HEALER. "YOUR ASSAILANT WAS A VERY POOR CRAFTSMAN. SEE, HE HELD THE BLADE THUS, AND IT COULD NOT GO BETWEEN YOUR RIBS," AND HE SHAKES HIS HEAD SADLY AT SUCH A SHODDY PERFORMANCE.

NOW NICILOS IS LEFT ALONE IN CHARGE OF THE CARAVAN AND IS IN A POSITION TO ROB HIS MASTER OF ALL HIS GOODS. SUCH AN OPPORTUNITY MIGHT NOT COME HIS WAY AGAIN.

1284.

BUT HE HESITATES. FAR OUT IN THE DESERT TALOON IS RIDING HOMEWARD TO HER DOOM.

9-17-61

TO HIS OWN ASTONISHMENT HE FINDS HE WANTS THE GIRL MORE THAN RICHES! HE STEALS BUT TWO HORSES AND RIDES IN PURSUIT.
NEXT WEEK-**The Meeting**

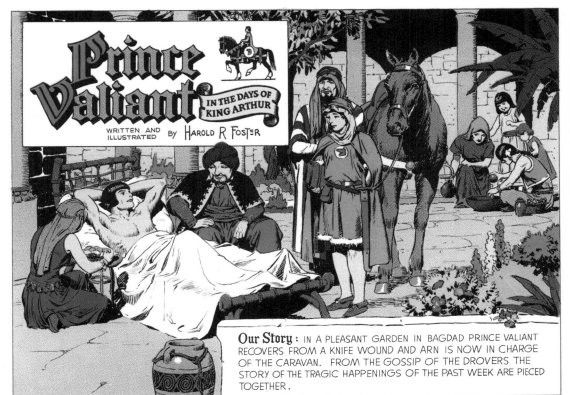

Prince Valiant
IN THE DAYS OF KING ARTHUR
WRITTEN AND ILLUSTRATED BY HAROLD R FOSTER

Our Story: IN A PLEASANT GARDEN IN BAGDAD PRINCE VALIANT RECOVERS FROM A KNIFE WOUND AND ARN IS NOW IN CHARGE OF THE CARAVAN. FROM THE GOSSIP OF THE DROVERS THE STORY OF THE TRAGIC HAPPENINGS OF THE PAST WEEK ARE PIECED TOGETHER.

AS A WOUNDED ANIMAL STRIVES TO REACH ITS LAIR, SO TALOON RIDES EASTWARD TOWARD THE WINDY STEPPES OF HER HOMELAND. SHE WOULD RATHER FACE THE DEATH SENTENCE THAT AWAITS HER THERE THAN LIVE IN THIS LAND.

AND NICILOS FOLLOWS, DRAWN ONWARD BY THE FIRST UNSELFISH LOVE HE HAS EVER KNOWN. HER TRAIL IS EASY TO FOLLOW, FOR AN UNVEILED WOMAN, RIDING ALONE, IS WORTHY OF NOTE.

NO HORSEMAN COULD OVERTAKE THE NIMBLE RIDER, BUT SHE MUST PAUSE OFTEN TO HUNT, AND AT NIGHT DESCEND TO THE VALLEYS TO RAID FIELD AND ORCHARD FOR FRUIT AND MELONS.

ON A MOUNTAIN PASS THEY MEET. "PRINCE VALIANT STILL LIVES," SAYS NICILOS AND WATCHES THE LOOK OF SORROW IN HER EYES TURN INTO RELIEF. "AND I LOVE YOU," HE ADDS.

AND CLEVER NICILOS, ONCE SO SLY AND GLIB, FINDS NO WORDS TO SAY AS HE LOOKS LONGINGLY AT THE PROUD, SELF-RELIANT GIRL BEFORE HIM.

1285.   9-24-61

TALOON RETURNS HIS GAZE. THEN THE CLOUDS SWEEP DOWN THE PASS AND THEY ARE OBSCURED IN MIST SO THAT NO ONE KNOWS HOW THEIR STORY ENDS.

NEXT WEEK—Belchad Abu

Prince Valiant
IN THE DAYS OF KING ARTHUR
WRITTEN AND ILLUSTRATED BY HAROLD R FOSTER

Our Story: SOON PRINCE VALIANT'S KNIFE WOUND BECOMES JUST ANOTHER SCAR AMONG THE MANY, AND HE BEGINS PLANNING THEIR HOMEWARD JOURNEY.

PLODDING HORSES ARE EXCHANGED FOR THE SWIFT CAMELS. VAL SIGHS WITH RELIEF WHEN ALL IS READY, FOR NOW THERE WILL BE NO MORE TEDIOUS BICKERING WITH SHREWD MERCHANTS.

ARN HAS HIS FIRST CAMEL RIDE AND LEARNS WHY THE ANIMAL IS CALLED THE 'SHIP OF THE DESERT'. HE BECOMES VIOLENTLY SEASICK!

THEIR CARAVAN IS LEFT FAR BEHIND AS THEY RIDE SWIFTLY UP THE EUPHRATES. AFTER SEVERAL DAYS THEY COME TO THE TOWN OF DEIR EZ ZOR, AND VAL REMEMBERS THIS PLACE ONLY TOO WELL.

"MY SON, DO YOU SEE YONDER FAT MERCHANT? THAT IS BELCHAD ABU. ONCE HE WORE THE 'SINGING SWORD' AND OWNED A SLAVE NAMED PRINCE VALIANT. WE WILL HAVE SOME FUN!"

AND SO THEY ARM THEMSELVES AND FOLLOW. AMONG ITS ORCHARDS AND GARDENS STANDS THE MERCHANT'S VILLA WHERE VAL HAD ONCE FELT THE STING OF THE LASH.

"WE FIND THE CARAVANSARY UNFIT TO ENTERTAIN ROYALTY, SO CRAVE YOUR HOSPITALITY FOR THE NIGHT." THE HAUGHTY MERCHANT LOOKS DISPLEASED WITH THIS INTRUSION UNTIL HIS EYE FALLS ON THE 'SINGING SWORD'. HE TAKES ANOTHER LOOK AT ITS OWNER AND HIS FACE GOES WHITE.

NEXT WEEK- **Out of the Past**

1286.

HAL FOSTER

10-1-61

Prince Valiant
IN THE DAYS OF KING ARTHUR

WRITTEN AND ILLUSTRATED BY HAROLD R FOSTER

Our Story: BELCHAD ABU LOOKS INTO THE GRINNING FACE OF HIS ONE-TIME SLAVE AND FEAR SHAKES HIM LIKE A LEAF. DOES THIS NOBLE PRINCE COME HERE TO SEEK REVENGE?

FOR WELL HE REMEMBERS THAT DAY IN DAMASCUS WHEN HE PURCHASED THE GREAT SWORD AND ITS OWNER FROM AN ARAB SLAVE DEALER.

"I AM PRINCE VALIANT, KNIGHT OF ARTHUR'S ROUND TABLE, HEIR TO THE KINGDOM OF THULE. WHEN, IN MY DISTANT HOMELAND, I HEARD TROUBADOURS TELL OF YOUR GREAT LOVELINESS, I TOOK SWORD AND SHIELD AND FOUGHT MY WAY ACROSS A THOUSAND LEAGUES OF HOSTILE LAND TO WIN TO YOUR SIDE!"

AND HOW THAT YOUNG SLAVE HAD RISKED DEATH BY ENTERING THE WOMEN'S QUARTERS AND MAKING SUCH ROMANTIC LOVE TO HIS DAUGHTER BERNICE THAT SHE HAD HELPED HIM ESCAPE.

SO VAL AND ARN TAKE THEIR EASE AND ENJOY THE DISCOMFITURE OF THEIR TREMBLING HOST. HIS GUEST HAS NO REASON TO LOVE HIM. HE ALSO HAS A BAD HABIT OF FONDLING HIS GLEAMING SWORD HILT. IT'S FRIGHTENING!

BERNICE HAS NEVER FORGOTTEN THE GALLANT LAD WHO HAD MADE LOVE TO HER SO LONG AGO. HE HAD BROKEN HER HEART THOUGH HE HAD NOT DESTROYED HER APPETITE. AND NOW SHE LEARNS HE HAS RETURNED.

"YOU HAVE COME BACK FOR ME," SHE PIPES. "I KNEW MY BEAUTY WOULD HAUNT YOU UNTIL YOU RETURNED." "HOLD!" CRIES VAL, "HAVE YOU FORGOTTEN THAT YOU HAD ME WHIPPED?"

"SILLY BOY," SHE COOS, "THAT WAS NOTHING. I ALWAYS HAVE MY SLAVES WHIPPED."

"YOU MUST HAVE BEEN A GAY BLADE IN YOUR YOUTH, SIRE," MUSES ARN. "DOES MOTHER KNOW SHE MARRIED A GREAT LOVER?"
"SHUT UP!" ANSWERS VAL.

NEXT WEEK—**Escape.**

1287.   10-8-61

Prince Valiant IN THE DAYS OF KING ARTHUR

WRITTEN AND ILLUSTRATED BY Harold R Foster

Our Story: BERNICE ARISES EARLY, THEN, DRESSED IN HER BEST AND SOAKED WITH PERFUME SHE PRACTICES SOME IRRESISTIBLE EXPRESSIONS IN HER MIRROR. FINALLY SHE IS READY TO MEET HER BELOVED.

BUT HER BELOVED HAS GONE, STRIDING AWAY IN THE DAWN WITH HIS YOUNG SON TROTTING BEHIND HIM.

PAMPERED AND SPOILED BERNICE HAS ALWAYS BEEN GIVEN WHAT SHE WANTED .....EXCEPT PRINCE VALIANT. AND, ALTHOUGH SHE SCREAMS AND RENDS HER GARMENTS, NONE OFFER TO BRING HIM BACK.

SHE SEEKS COMFORT BY FLINGING HERSELF INTO HER FATHER'S ARMS .....BUT SHE HAS PUT ON WEIGHT SINCE LAST SHE DID THIS. THEN, SO EVERYONE MIGHT SHARE HER SORROW, SHE ORDERS FIVE LASHES APIECE TO THE SLAVES....AND FEELS MUCH BETTER.

PRINCE VALIANT COMES ROARING INTO THE CARAVANSARY AND ORDERS THE CAMEL MEN TO SADDLE THE ANIMALS AND GET MOVING, FAST.

"AND YOU, MY SON, MENTION ONE WORD OF THIS TO YOUR MOTHER, AND I'LL SKIN YOU ALIVE!"
"BUT, SIRE, YOU KNOW WHAT A LOOSE TONGUE I HAVE."

"THOUGH A BRIGHT NEW DAMASCUS BLADE MIGHT BE OF SUCH IMPORTANCE TO ME THAT I WOULD FORGET ALL LESSER TRIFLES."
"A BLACKMAILER!" MUSES VAL APPROVINGLY.

ALONG THE ROUTE THEY MUST TAKE, A REAL BLACKMAILER AWAITS THE DOOM HE HAS TRULY EARNED, AND PRAYS THAT SOME MIRACLE WILL SAVE HIM.

NEXT WEEK- **Alimann 'the cruel'**

1288. 10-15-61

Prince Valiant
IN THE DAYS OF KING ARTHUR
WRITTEN AND ILLUSTRATED BY HAROLD R FOSTER

Our Story: ALIMANN HAS COMMITTED MANY CRIMES THAT WOULD BRING SHAME TO A LESS EVIL MAN, BUT NOW HE HAS GONE TOO FAR. HIS LATEST DEED MIGHT BRING VENGEANCE, SWIFT AND TERRIBLE, OUT OF THE DESERT.

HE HAD BEEN CAREFUL THAT HIS THIEVING RAIDS WERE MADE FAR FROM HOME, BUT, FROM HIS HILL FORT, HE HAD SEEN ALL THE MEN FROM A NEARBY OASIS VILLAGE RIDE TO THE CONCLAVE IN DEIR EZ ZOR.

THE TEMPTATION WAS TOO GREAT AND HE HAD RAIDED THE HELPLESS VILLAGE. AND NOW, AS HE SEES THE DESERT MEN RETURNING, HE WONDERS IF HIS MEN HAVE LEFT ANYONE ALIVE WHO MIGHT BE SNEAKY ENOUGH TO TELL ON HIM.

OH! HOW HE WISHES HE HAD MORE SWORDSMEN WITHIN HIS STRONGHOLD! AS IF IN ANSWER TO HIS PRAYER A KNIGHT WITH ARMED GUARDS RIDES BY, AND HE SENDS OUT AN INVITATION.

PRINCE VALIANT, ARN AND THEIR CAMEL GUARD ACCEPT ALIMANN'S HOSPITALITY. IF ATTACK COMES DURING THE NIGHT, THE GUESTS WILL ALSO HAVE TO FIGHT FOR THEIR LIVES, AND EVERY SWORD COUNTS.

BEFORE DAWN ALIMANN AWAKES ONE OF VAL'S CAMEL GUARDS. THERE ARE WHISPERED WORDS AND A PURSE OF MONEY CHANGES HANDS.

AS VAL LEAVES EARLY HE IS NOT SURPRISED THAT ALIMANN IS NOT THERE TO BID THEM FARE-WELL, SO HE LEAVES A MESSAGE OF THANKS AND GOES HIS WAY.

TOWARD EVENING A TROOP OF HORSEMEN OVER-TAKES THEM AND VAL LOOSENS THE 'SINGING SWORD' IN ITS SCABBARD AND TAKES HIS SHIELD.
NEXT WEEK— **The Stowaway**

1289.

10-22-61

Prince Valiant
IN THE DAYS OF KING ARTHUR
WRITTEN AND ILLUSTRATED BY HAROLD R FOSTER

Our Story: THE DESERT MEN GALLOP UP AND SURROUND PRINCE VALIANT, ARN AND THE TWO GUARDS. "WE SEARCH FOR 'ALIMANN THE CRUEL'," SAYS THEIR CHIEFTAIN. "WE LEARNED THAT YOU STAYED THE NIGHT WITH HIM."

"WE WERE GUESTS IN THE STRONGHOLD OF ALIMANN LAST NIGHT BUT LEFT EARLY THIS MORNING WITHOUT SEEING OUR HOST. WHY DO YOU SEARCH FOR HIM?"

"WHEN WE RETURNED TO OUR VILLAGE IT WAS IN RUINS. OUR PARENTS, OUR WIVES AND CHILDREN ALL SLAIN, OUR HOMES PLUNDERED. SUCH IS THE WORK OF 'ALIMANN THE CRUEL'".

"AND TO THINK WE ATE AND DRANK WITH SUCH A MONSTER!" EXCLAIMS VAL. "BUT, AS YOU CAN SEE, HE DOES NOT RIDE WITH US."

BUT THAT EVENING WHEN THE BAGGAGE CAMEL IS UNLOADED IT SEEMS THAT ALIMANN DOES RIDE WITH THEM!

KNIGHTS OF THE ROUND TABLE MUST BE JUDGE, JURY AND EXECUTIONER, IF NEED BE, BUT SHOULD VAL SOIL THE 'SINGING SWORD' ON SUCH CARRION?

ALIMANN BACKS AWAY. IF HE CAN SEIZE THE BOY AS A HOSTAGE.......BUT ARN IS LEARNING HIS TRADE WELL AND IS PREPARED.

1290.

THEN HE RUNS. ACROSS THE DARKENING DESERT HE RUNS WITH HIS COMPANION, FEAR!
NEXT WEEK— **Homecoming**

10-29-61

Prince Valiant
IN THE DAYS OF KING ARTHUR
WRITTEN AND ILLUSTRATED BY HAROLD R. FOSTER

Our Story : PRINCE VALIANT WATCHES ALIMANN 'THE CRUEL' RUN, PANIC-STRICKEN, OUT INTO THE DARKENING DESERT AND SHEATHES THE 'SINGING SWORD'.

HOW ARROGANT HE HAD BEEN AS HE RODE THESE SAME PLAINS SURROUNDED BY HIS CUTTHROAT BAND! NOW HE IS ALONE, EVERY MAN AN ENEMY.

WHEN DAY COMES HE HIDES IN A WADI AND, UNDER THE DESERT SUN, LEARNS THE HORRORS OF THIRST.

THE SONS, THE FATHERS AND THE HUSBANDS OF HIS VICTIMS THIRST FOR HIS BLOOD; ONLY WITHIN HIS STRONGHOLD CAN HE HOPE FOR SAFETY.

AT LAST! HE KNOCKS ON THE GATE: "OPEN", HE WHISPERS, "IT IS I, ALIMANN!"

THE GATES OPEN AND HE RUNS TOWARD HIS LIGHTED HALL, SCREAMING ORDERS TO THE SHADOWY FIGURES TO REDOUBLE THEIR WATCH.

ALIMANN, THE CRUEL, AT LAST COMES HOME. AND THERE WAITING FOR HIM ARE THOSE HE FEARS MOST, THE DESERT TRIBE WHOSE VILLAGE HE HAD SO TERRIBLY RAVISHED!

NEXT WEEK - **Sound and Fury**

HAL FOSTER

1291.

11-5-61

Our Story: FOR WEEKS PRINCE VALIANT HAS FOLLOWED THE BANKS OF THE EUPHRATES, BUT NOW THEY LEAVE THE RIVER AND CROSS OVER THE BARREN HEIGHT OF LAND.

THEN DOWN INTO THE GREEN VALLEY AND ALEPPO, WHERE THE CARAVAN ROUTES CONVERGE. AND VAL HASTENS TO COLLECT THE LETTERS THAT AWAIT HIM THERE.

ALETA WRITES THAT HIS VENTURE INTO TRADE HAS BEEN A GREAT SUCCESS; THAT HER SHIPS ARE CARRYING AN INCREASING AMOUNT OF TRADE GOODS AND THAT HE MUST HURRY HOME. IN FACT, BOLTAR IS EVEN NOW AWAITING HIM IN THE HARBOR OF ANTIOCH.

EAGER AS A SCHOOLBOY VAL RACES TO ANTIOCH TO FIND BOLTAR. THIS IS EASY, AS THE ROAR OF HIS VOICE CAN BE HEARD ABOVE THE TUMULT OF THE BUSY PORT.

BOLTAR, HIS GREAT AXE IN HAND, IS DARING THE HARBOR GUARD TO TRY TO ARREST HIM OR HIS MEN.

VAL RIDES ALONG THE EDGE OF THE QUAY UNTIL EVEN WITH BOLTAR'S SHIP. THEN HE BECKONS THE SAILORS TO LOAD THEIR GEAR WHILE HE PAYS OFF THE CAMEL MEN.

BOLTAR COMES ABOARD GRUMBLING LIKE AN ANGRY VOLCANO. "THE MANGY, FLEA-BITTEN MERCHANTS OF THIS TOWN WILL GET NO MORE OF MY TRADE!"

"I LET MY LADS GO ASHORE FOR A FROLIC. YOU KNOW BOYS WILL BE BOYS. NOW THE UNCOUTH SHOPKEEPERS WANT ME TO PAY DAMAGES!" AND HE SHAKES HIS HEAD AT THE INJUSTICE OF IT ALL.

NEXT WEEK - The Queen

1292.

11-12-61

Prince Valiant
IN THE DAYS OF KING ARTHUR
WRITTEN AND ILLUSTRATED BY HAROLD R FOSTER

Our Story: ALETA, QUEEN OF THE MISTY ISLES, HAS SENT BOLTAR TO BRING PRINCE VALIANT AND ARN OUT OF THE NEAR EAST AND IT IS QUITE EVIDENT THAT THE SLEEK DRAGONSHIP HAS SAILED THESE WATERS BEFORE. MERCHANT SHIPS SCUTTLE FOR THE SAFETY OF THE NEAREST PORT WHERE SPEARMEN HASTILY MAN THE BATTLEMENTS.

"DID YOU EVER SEE SUCH SUSPICIOUS PEOPLE?" GRUMBLES BOLTAR. "THEIR LACK OF TRUST GIVES ME THAT UNWANTED FEELING."

ONCE AGAIN VAL RETURNS TO A CHANGED WIFE, MORE MATURE NOW, POISED AND SERENE. HOW DIFFERENT FROM THE YOUNG QUEEN WHO HAD LOST A SLIPPER IN A WILD RUSH TO FLING HERSELF INTO HIS ARMS! SHE COMES TO MEET HIM SLOWLY AS IF TO PROLONG THE JOY OF GREETING.

SHE IS, IF POSSIBLE, LOVELIER THAN EVER. HIS EYES ARE BIG WITH WONDER, HIS HANDS TREMBLE AND HE FINDS NO WORDS TO SAY. ALETA SMILES CONTENTEDLY, THE DEAR BOY HAS NOT CHANGED A BIT!

HOW CAN A MAN EVER LEARN TO UNDERSTAND A WOMAN WHO KEEPS CHANGING ALL THE TIME? IT IS NOT RECORDED THAT HE EVER FOUND AN ANSWER TO THE QUESTION.

AT LAST PRINCE ARN HAS AN AUDIENCE TO LISTEN TO HIS TALES OF ADVENTURE AND THE WONDERS HE HAS SEEN. AND VAL SPENDS JOYOUS HOURS WITH HIS FAMILY, HOURS THAT ARE DOUBLY PRECIOUS FOR THEY COME ALL TOO SELDOM IN THE LIFE OF A PRACTICING WARRIOR.

NEXT WEEK- A Royal Error

1293.

11-19-61

Our Story: PRINCE VALIANT WATCHES HIS WIFE IN AMAZEMENT. WHO WOULD THINK THAT SUCH A PRETTY LITTLE HEAD COULD CONTAIN SUCH MATURE WISDOM? SHE HAS BECOME TRULY A QUEEN WHOSE AUTHORITY IS UNQUESTIONED.

EVEN IN THE COUNCIL OF ELDERS, USUALLY LOUD WITH DEBATE, HER POLICIES ARE ACCEPTED, HER COMMANDS CARRIED OUT.

IN FACT, SHE HAS BECOME SO USED TO AUTHORITY THAT SHE GIVES ORDERS TO HER HUSBAND. IN THE BRITTLE SILENCE THAT FOLLOWS SHE REALIZES HER MISTAKE.

SHE QUICKLY SHIFTS TO HER OWN TRIED AND TRUE FORM OF DIPLOMACY AND THE ANGRY GLINT IN VAL'S EYE SOFTENS. ALETA WILL, OF COURSE, GET HER OWN WAY BUT BY A MUCH SWEETER METHOD.

A SHIP COMES TO THE MISTY ISLES BEARING A WOUNDED KNIGHT WHO ASKS TO BE BORNE TO THE PALACE.

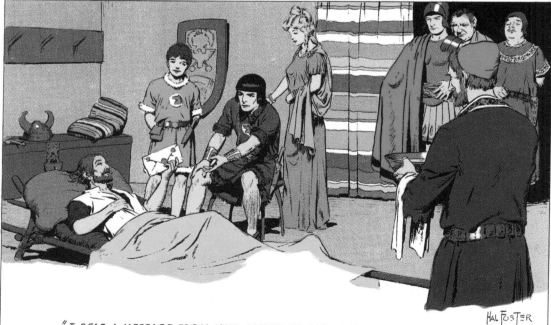

"I BEAR A MESSAGE FROM KING ARTHUR TO PRINCE VALIANT. OF THE FOUR KNIGHTS IN OUR PARTY ONLY I SURVIVED THE JOURNEY THROUGH GAUL."

NEXT WEEK- **The Courier**

1294.

11-26-61

Our Story: KING ARTHUR CALLED FOUR KNIGHTS BEFORE HIM AND SAID: *"CARRY THIS MESSAGE TO PRINCE VALIANT IN THE MISTY ISLES. I SEND FOUR OF YOU AS THE WAY ACROSS GAUL IS PERILOUS AND ONE OF YOU MUST GET THROUGH."*

ONLY SIR GOSFORTH SURVIVED AND HE SORELY WOUNDED. FROM HIS BREAST HE TAKES A LETTER AND HANDS IT TO PRINCE VALIANT.

"YOU, SIR VALIANT, ARE BEST EQUIPPED TO BE OUR AMBASSADOR TO ROME", WROTE ARTHUR. *"GO TO THEIR EMPEROR IN HIS PALACE AND BESEECH HIS HELP IN OPENING THE ROAD THROUGH GAUL, ELSE CHRISTIAN BRITAIN BE CUT OFF FROM THE REST OF CHRISTENDOM."*

"WHEN I HAVE FINISHED MY MISSION TO ROME I MUST RETURN TO CAMELOT TO REPORT MY SUCCESS... OR FAILURE." ALETA SMILES: *"I HAVE ALREADY PREPARED MY GOVERNMENT TO FUNCTION IN MY ABSENCE, FOR I GO WITH YOU."*

"AND IT WILL BE A GREAT BUSINESS VENTURE, FOR WE WILL GO IN A FLEET OF SHIPS LOADED WITH GOODS, AND TRADE FOR TIN, FURS, AMBER AND GOLD. IF GAUL IS CLOSED, WE WILL OPEN A SEA ROUTE!"

VAL AND ARN DEPART IN BOLTAR'S LONG-SHIP TO COMPLETE HIS MISSION AND RENDEZVOUS WITH THE FLEET AT GIBRALTAR.

QUEEN ALETA LEAVES HER HAPPY LITTLE KINGDOM. IN HER SHORT STAY STRONG WALLS HAVE BEEN BUILT, AN INVASION CRUSHED, AND A CAPTURED FLEET IS BRINGING IN RICHES.
THE MISTY ISLES FADE INTO THE DISTANCE AND SHE IS NO LONGER A QUEEN, ONLY MADAM VALIANT, BUT SHE IS CONTENT.

NEXT WEEK – **Rome**

1295.

HAL FOSTER

12-3-61

Prince Valiant

IN THE DAYS OF KING ARTHUR

WRITTEN AND ILLUSTRATED BY HAROLD R FOSTER

Our Story: BOLTAR'S SHIP LANDS AT OSTIA AND PRINCE VALIANT AND ARN TAKE THE ROAD TO ROME. THEY RIDE BY FIELDS CHOKED WITH WEEDS, RUINED VILLAS; EVEN THE TOMBS OF FAMOUS GENERALS ARE LOOTED AND DEFACED. THE FEW PEOPLE THEY MEET ARE IN RAGS.

AS THEY ENTER THE GATES ARN GASPS: "THE TEMPLES AND PALACES OF ROME MAKE HER THE QUEEN CITY OF THE WORLD!" THEN HE ADDS, "BUT THE BEGGARS OF BAGDAD WERE BETTER CLOTHED THAN ROMAN CITIZENS!"

THEN THEY FIND LODGINGS IN A PALACE. SO OFTEN HAS IT BEEN PILLAGED THAT ITS PATRICIAN OWNER IS GLAD TO TAKE IN PAYING GUESTS.

NOW BEGINS VAL'S EFFORT TO SEE THE EMPEROR. ONLY WITH BRIBES CAN HE GET FROM DOORMAN UP TO CHAMBERLAIN. IT WILL COST A FORTUNE TO REACH HIS GOAL.

VAL IS NOT USED TO THESE MEAN WAYS. HE FEELS DEGRADED AND TELLS OF HIS DISAPPOINTMENT TO HIS GENTLE HOST.

1296.

"I STILL RETAIN SOCIAL POSITION AND SOME SMALL INFLUENCE AND COULD INVITE GUESTS HIGH IN GOVERNMENT TO A BANQUET." HE HOLDS HIS HEAD PROUDLY TO OVERCOME HIS SHAME AS HE ADDS, " YOU WILL HAVE TO PAY THE COST, I CAN NO LONGER AFFORD IT."

ROME IS LIKE A BEAUTIFUL LADY WHO, GROWN CARELESS IN HER WAYS, WITH DIRTY FACE AND TORN GARMENTS, AWAITS FURTHER MISFORTUNE.
NEXT WEEK- **The Ruined Queen**

HAL FOSTER

12-10-61

Prince Valiant
IN THE DAYS OF KING ARTHUR
WRITTEN AND ILLUSTRATED BY HAROLD R FOSTER

Our Story : PRINCE VALIANT AND HIS HOST ARRANGE A BANQUET SO THAT VAL MAY MEET SOME INFLUENTIAL MEN IN GOVERNMENT AND THROUGH THEM GET AN AUDIENCE WITH THE EMPEROR.

THE STREETS OF ROME TELL ARN A SAD STORY. POVERTY IS THE LOT OF ITS PEOPLE, AND GROUPS OF BARBARIANS WANDER ABOUT AT WILL SEEKING PLEASURE.

TWO GRACEFUL PILLARS OF MARBLE, INTRICATELY CARVED, STAND BEFORE A RUINED PALACE. WITH GREAT SHOUTING AND LAUGHTER THE GOTHS ARE HEAVING ON ROPES FLUNG OVER THE TOP.

AT LAST THE SLENDER COLUMNS TOPPLE AND, WITH A THUNDEROUS ROAR, ARE REDUCED TO RUBBLE. AT THIS THE BARBARIANS SHRIEK WITH DELIGHT FOR, UNABLE TO CREATE BEAUTY THEMSELVES, THEY TAKE JOY IN ITS DESTRUCTION!

BEYOND A GARDEN WALL A SMALL SWEET VOICE IS SINGING. ONLY A VERY BEAUTIFUL GARDEN COULD INSPIRE SUCH A HAPPY SONG AND ARN WOULD LIKE TO SEE IT. HE CAN, IN FACT, FOR THE WINDOW OF A RUINED BUILDING OVERLOOKS THE GARDEN.

BUT HERE IS A MYSTERY. THERE IS CERTAINLY A WINDOW ON THE OUTSIDE, BUT NONE INSIDE! OR COULD THERE BE A SECRET PASSAGE ?

HE CLIMBS TO THE TOP, AND THERE, SURE ENOUGH, IS A STAIRWAY WITHIN THE THICKNESS OF THE WALL -- AND A WINDOW.

1297.

HAL FOSTER

THE FOLIAGE IS SO HIGH HE CAN ONLY SEE THE TOP OF A MARBLE PAVILION. THE STAIRS CONTINUE DOWNWARD AND A FAINT GLEAM OF LIGHT MAY MEAN A DOORWAY.

NEXT WEEK - The Enchanted Garden

12-17-61

Our Story: PRINCE ARN DESCENDS THE SECRET STAIRWAY CAREFULLY, THE WOODEN DOOR AT THE BOTTOM CRUMBLES IN HIS HAND AND A KICK BREAKS THE RUSTED LOCK ON THE IRON GRILL. THEN HE IS IN THE GARDEN.

A WILDERNESS OF WEEDS AND BRAMBLES GREETS HIM, BUT A PAVED WALK CREATES A TUNNEL THROUGH WHICH HE CRAWLS.

ARN EMERGES INTO A WELL-KEPT GARDEN, BRIGHT WITH FLOWERS. *"I HEARD YOU COMING,"* CALLS A VOICE, *"ARE YOU A PRINCE?"*

"YES, I AM PRINCE ARN."
"AND DO YOU RIDE A WHITE HORSE?" SHE ASKS.
"YES, I HAVE A WHITE HORSE AT CAMELOT."
"THEN YOU HAVE COME TO RESCUE ME FROM OUT OF THIS ENCHANTED GARDEN!"

"FOR ONLY A PRINCE ON A WHITE HORSE CAN BREAK THE SPELL OF THE EVIL SORCERESS WHO KEEPS ME IMPRISONED." WHAT A STRANGE LITTLE ELF THIS IS, THINKS ARN, NOT ONCE HAS SHE LOOKED AT ME.

"SO, YESTERDAY I WAS A GOOD FAIRY; TODAY I AM AN EVIL WITCH! WELL, FOR NOW I AM JUST YOUR OLD NANA AND HAVE LAID OUT YOUR LUNCH."

1298.

"YOU SEE HOW SHE CHANGES? IT IS MAGIC," AND THE GIRL REACHES FOR HIM, MISSES, TRIES AGAIN AND CATCHES HIS SLEEVE. *"COME ON,"* SHE SAYS.

ONLY THEN DOES ARN REALIZE THAT SHE IS BLIND. BLIND BUT LIVING IN A BEAUTIFUL WORLD OF FANTASY.
NEXT WEEK-
The World behind the Garden Wall.

12-24-61

Prince Valiant

IN THE DAYS OF KING ARTHUR

WRITTEN AND ILLUSTRATED By HAROLD R FOSTER

Our Story: SEEKING ADVENTURE, PRINCE ARN FOLLOWS A SECRET PASSAGE AND COMES TO AN ENCHANTED GARDEN. HERE A BLIND PRINCESS IS WAITING TO BE RESCUED FROM A WITCH. BUT THE WITCH CALLS THEM TO LUNCH, SO THE ESCAPE IS POSTPONED.

SHE LEADS ARN BY THE HAND. *"THE PATH IS HERE,"* SHE INSTRUCTS, *"NOW WE COME TO THREE STEPS, NOW THE PATH TURNS....."* ARN HAS THE STRANGE FEELING THAT HE IS ACTUALLY LIVING IN A FAIRY TALE.

THEN HE MAKES A DISCOVERY. NOT ONLY IS THE SMALL MISS BLIND, BUT SHE HAS NEVER BEEN TOLD THAT OTHERS CAN SEE!

"MY MOTHER IS COMING, SHE IS VERY BEAUTIFUL," ANNOUNCES THE PRINCESS, *"AND THUMP, THUMP, THUMP, HERE COMES MY FATHER."* THEN SHE WHISPERS: *"I AM REALLY NOT A PRINCESS, BUT I WILL BE WHEN MY FATHER IS EMPEROR."*

"HOW DID THIS BOY GET INTO THE GARDEN AND WHO IS HE?" DEMANDS THE FATHER.

"I AM PRINCE ARN, SON OF SIR VALIANT, AND I CAME BY WAY OF A SECRET PASSAGE AMONG THE BRIARS AT THE FOOT OF THE GARDEN," ANSWERS ARN.

"SIR VALIANT?" MUSES THE FATHER, *"ISN'T HE THE KNIGHT WHO IS TRYING TO GAIN AUDIENCE WITH THE EMPEROR ON BEHALF OF KING ARTHUR OF BRITAIN?"*

1299.

ARN TELLS OF HIS SIRE'S MISSION AND THE DIFFICULTIES HE MEETS IN HIS EFFORT TO REACH THE EMPEROR. ONLY WHEN THE TALE IS TOLD DOES THE BLIND GIRL SPEAK:

12-31-61

"NOW LET THE PRINCE TELL OF HIS TRAVELS TO FABULOUS CATHAY AND THE MAGIC ISLES OF SPICE; OF THE WONDROUS ADVENTURES HE HAS HAD AND THE STRANGE PEOPLE HE HAS MET!"
NEXT WEEK- **The Story Teller**

Prince Valiant

IN THE DAYS OF KING ARTHUR

WRITTEN AND ILLUSTRATED By HAROLD R FOSTER

Our Story : PRINCE ARN DISCOVERS A SECRET PASSAGE AND ENTERS A GARDEN, THE ABODE OF A LITTLE BLIND GIRL, WHO BELIEVES IN FAIRY TALES.

"COME, PRINCE ARN, SHOW ME THIS HIDDEN ENTRANCE," SAYS HER FATHER.

"YES, LAD, I KNOW OF THIS GATE AND I MUST REPAIR IT. I BROUGHT YOU AWAY TO ASK YOU TO GUARD WELL YOUR TONGUE WHEN YOU SPEAK TO MY DAUGHTER."

"FOR HER DAYS ARE NUMBERED AND THEY ARE FEW. WE STRIVE TO MAKE THOSE DAYS HAPPY, AND SO HAVE NOT TOLD HER SHE IS BLIND OR THAT OTHERS ARE MORE FORTUNATE."

THE CHILD'S SIGHTLESS EYES GROW BIG WITH WONDER AS ARN TELLS THE SAGAS OF THE NORSE HEROES. IT IS EASY TO BELIEVE THIS IS AN ENCHANTED GARDEN AND AT ANY MOMENT A FAIRY OR ELF MAY APPEAR.

THE OLD NANA BREAKS THE SPELL: *"COME, CHILD, YOU HAVE HAD ENOUGH EXCITEMENT FOR THE DAY AND IT IS TIME FOR YOUR REST."*

AS ARN LEAVES THE VILLA THE FATHER STOPS HIM. *"YOU HAVE BROUGHT PLEASURE TO MY DAUGHTER. IN GRATITUDE I MIGHT SAVE THE NOBLE SIR VALIANT MUCH TROUBLE. SEND HIM TO ME."*

1300.

ARN HASTENS TO THEIR LODGINGS BUT HIS FATHER IS WELCOMING THE GUESTS ARRIVING FOR THE BANQUET, AND HE WILL HAVE TO WITHHOLD THE OFFER UNTIL THE MORROW.

NEXT WEEK- **The Banquet**

HAL FOSTER

1-7-62

Our Story RETURNS TO PRINCE VALIANT AND HIS EFFORTS TO REACH THE EMPEROR. HIS KINDLY HOST HAS SPREAD A BANQUET AND INVITED AS GUESTS MEN HIGH IN GOVERNMENT IN THE HOPE THEY MIGHT AID VAL IN HIS QUEST.

BUT WHEN VAL MAKES MENTION OF HIS PROJECT THEY ADROITLY TURN THE CONVERSATION. THEY WOULD HELP NO ONE BUT THEMSELVES. THAT THEY HAD HELPED THEMSELVES IS EVIDENT BY THEIR WEALTH.

THE REPARTEE IS WITTY, THE CONVERSATION BRILLIANT, BUT ANY MENTION OF POLITICS IS AVOIDED AS IF IT WERE SOMETHING MENACING THEY WISHED TO FORGET.

WHEN, AT DAWN, THE BANQUET ENDS, VAL KNOWS ONE THING: THAT DESPITE THE GAIETY AND LOUD LAUGHTER THESE MEN DISTRUST AND FEAR EACH OTHER.

"MY PLAN WAS ONLY AN EXPENSIVE FAILURE," SAYS HIS HOST. "I HAVE THE IMPRESSION MY FRIENDS WOULD RATHER PREVENT THAN HELP YOU MEET THE EMPEROR."

1301.

ARN OFFERS A RAY OF HOPE. "I MADE FRIENDS WITH A LITTLE BLIND GIRL, AND HER FATHER TOLD ME HE MIGHT BE OF SERVICE TO YOU."

VAL IS WILLING TO TRY ANYTHING THAT WILL BRING HIS PETITION BEFORE THE EMPEROR, SO HE BIDS ARN LEAD THE WAY.

NEXT WEEK **The Doomed City**

1-14-62

Prince Valiant
IN THE DAYS OF KING ARTHUR
WRITTEN AND ILLUSTRATED BY HAROLD R FOSTER

Our Story: PRINCE VALIANT FOLLOWS HIS SON TO THE HOME OF MARCUS SEVERIS WHO HAS PROMISED HIM AID. THE LITTLE BLIND GIRL TAKES ARN TO THE GARDEN TO LISTEN TO HIS WONDROUS TALES AND HER FATHER SEATS VAL ON THE PATIO.

"MY MISSION IS SIMPLE. UNLESS THE ROAD THROUGH GAUL IS OPENED, CHRISTIAN BRITAIN WILL BE CUT OFF FROM THE REST OF CHRISTENDOM. KING ARTHUR REQUESTS AID FROM THE EMPEROR OF ROME."

"YOU WILL NEVER DELIVER YOUR PETITION," SAYS MARCUS QUIETLY. "THE EMPEROR IS SURROUNDED BY FAWNING POLITICIANS, EACH SEEKING HIS FAVOR. WHO AMONG THEM WOULD RISK HIS POSITION BY INTRODUCING SO UNPLEASANT A SUBJECT AS AID? ROME CANNOT EVEN PROTECT ITS OWN WALLS!"

"OUR LEGIONS COULD NOT PREVENT THE GOTHS FROM CROSSING THE MIGHTY RHINE. HOW COULD THEY BE EXPECTED TO HOLD A NARROW RIBBON OF ROAD? THE GOTHS HAVE SPREAD OVER EUROPE, OTHER TRIBES FOLLOW AND THIS FORWARD MOVEMENT EXTENDS AS FAR BACK AS THE BALTIC."

"ROME IS DOOMED! WHO WOULD FIGHT FOR HER? THE POPULACE STARVES, THE WEALTH AND POWER IS IN THE HANDS OF A SELFISH FEW. BEYOND OUR BORDERS BARBARIAN CHIEFTAINS ALREADY GAZE OUR WAY."

"MY MISSION THEN IS A FAILURE AND IT IS SAD NEWS I MUST BRING TO MY KING."

1302.

A LOOK OF SADNESS COMES TO THE GIRL'S SIGHTLESS EYES AS ARN BIDS HER FAREWELL. "BE PATIENT," HE SAYS, "FOR I SAIL IN A VIKING DRAGONSHIP FAR TO THE NORTH, WHERE THE WILD GEESE GO. IF CHANCE BRINGS ME THIS WAY AGAIN I'LL HAVE MANY NEW TALES TO TELL."

NEXT WEEK- **New Plans**

1-21-62

HAL FOSTER

Our Story: PRINCE VALIANT RIDES AWAY FROM ROME, HIS MISSION A FAILURE. BUT ARN LOOKS BACK OFTEN TO WHERE THE CITY CROWNS ITS SEVEN HILLS, THE MORNING SUN SHINING ON ITS MARBLE PALACES AND THE SQUALOR AND POVERTY OF ITS STREETS HIDDEN. IT HAD BEEN FORETOLD THAT THE BARBARIANS WOULD ONCE MORE DESTROY IT, BUT WOULD IT DIE AS DID BABYLON, OR RETURN AGAIN AS 'THE ETERNAL CITY'?

ON BOLTAR'S LONGSHIP THEY SAIL TO RENDEZVOUS WITH ALETA'S FLEET. VAL HAS BOUGHT MANY MAPS IN ROME AND THESE HE STUDIES FOR HOURS AT A TIME. A PLAN IS FORMING.

A FAIR WIND BRINGS THEM TO THE ISLAND OF MENORCA AND THERE, IN A SHELTERED BAY, LIES ALETA'S FLEET OF SHIPS, STORM-DRIVEN OFF THEIR COURSE AND AWAITING A FAVORABLE BREEZE.

THIS IS GREAT GOOD FORTUNE, FOR NOT ONLY ARE THEY TOGETHER AGAIN WEEKS SOONER, BUT FROM HERE VAL CAN PUT HIS PLANS INTO ACTION, AND THEY ARE BOLD PLANS.

HE PINS ONE OF HIS MAPS ON THE WALL AND WITH RED CHALK DRAWS A LINE. *"THIS IS THE PRESENT ROUTE FROM HERE TO BRITAIN,"* HE SAYS. THEN WITH BLUE CHALK TRACES ANOTHER LINE. *"THIS IS THE NEW WAY I PROPOSE TO EXPLORE. IF AN OVERLAND ROAD CAN BE BUILT, IT WILL SAVE MORE THAN A THOUSAND MILES OF SEA VOYAGE!"*

1303.

ONCE MORE VAL AND PRINCE ARN SET OFF AT ADVENTURE. ALETA SIGHS. OH, WELL, SHE WON'T BE LONELY, FOR HER HUSBAND HAS LEFT HER WITH THREE CHILDREN TO LOOK AFTER.

NEXT WEEK- **Hispania**

1-28-62

Our Story: WHERE THE PYRENEES MOUNTAINS COME DOWN TO THE SEA THERE IS A TOWN, AND HERE PRINCE VALIANT GOES ASHORE. TO THE SOUTH LIES HISPANIA (SPAIN), ON THE NORTH GAUL (FRANCE). HE SECURES HORSES AND A GUIDE.

THE TRAIL IS STEEP AND ROUGH, UNFIT FOR THE TRADE ROUTE FROM SEA TO SEA HE WISHES TO ESTABLISH.

"SUCH A ROAD IS POSSIBLE TO THE SOUTH, BUT THE VISIGOTHS OVERRUN THE LAND AND AN ARMY COULD NOT KEEP THE WAY SAFE," THEIR GUIDE TELLS THEM.

"THERE IS A ROAD IN THE SOUTH OF GAUL THAT FOLLOWS THE GARONNE RIVER. WAR IS INCESSANT THERE AND POWERFUL CHIEFTAINS ARE BUILDING STRONG WALLS OF STONE AND TALL CASTLES TO DEFEND WHAT THEY CLAIM IS THEIRS."

VAL AND ARN STUDY THEIR CRUDE MAPS AND DECIDE TO LEAVE THE MOUNTAINS AND TRAVERSE THE LESS RUGGED FOOTHILLS.

JUSTIN HAD TAKEN HIS FATHER'S SWORD AND SHIRT OF MAIL AND GONE OFF TO WAR. NOW, TWO YEARS LATER, HE RETURNS HOMEWARD, RICHER ONLY BY HIS SCARS.

1304.

NUMBLY HE SITS AMID THE WRECKAGE OF HIS FATHER'S HOUSE. HE KNOWS ONLY TOO WELL, FROM GRIM EXPERIENCE, WHAT HAPPENS TO A VILLAGE WHEN WAR COMES.

HE IS AROUSED FROM DESPAIR BY THE SMELL OF FOOD. HIS NOSE, SHARPENED BY MONTHS OF HUNGER, LEADS HIM TO THE SOURCE. QUIETLY HE DRAWS HIS SWORD.

NEXT WEEK - The Demon

2-4-62

Prince Valiant
IN THE DAYS OF KING ARTHUR
WRITTEN AND ILLUSTRATED BY Harold R Foster

Our Story: PRINCE VALIANT PULLS UP HIS COIF AND DRAWS THE 'SINGING SWORD' AS THE ARMED WARRIOR APPROACHES. LINES OF SORROW AND DESPAIR ARE ETCHED ON HIS FACE AND HIS HUNGRY EYES STARE AT THE FOOD.

VAL LOWERS HIS SWORD POINT, THE SOLDIER DOES LIKEWISE. THEN VAL SHIFTS HIS WEAPON TO HIS LEFT HAND AND RAISES HIS RIGHT PALM OUT. THE SOLDIER FOLLOWS SUIT, THE SIGN OF PEACE.

VAL SHEATHES HIS SWORD AND WITH A WAVE OF HIS HAND INVITES THE MAN TO SHARE HIS REPAST. THERE CAN BE NO DOUBT THAT HE IS ON THE VERGE OF STARVATION.

ONLY WHEN HIS HUNGER IS SATISFIED DOES HE TALK. THEN, POINTING TO THE LUSH LANDS BELOW THEM, HE TELLS OF INCESSANT WARS, BRUTAL AND RUINOUS; OF CHIEFTAINS LEAVING THEIR STRONG-HOLDS TO LAY WASTE THE HOLDINGS OF THEIR NEIGHBORS.

THEIR GUIDE REFUSES TO GO FARTHER. HE PREFERS THE DOUBTFUL SAFETY OF THE RUG-GED MOUNTAINS TO THE CERTAINTY OF BEING MURDERED IN THE LOWLANDS.

SO THE GUIDE IS PAID OFF AND JUSTIN VOL-UNTEERS TO TAKE HIS PLACE. AFTER THE DULL MISERY OF WARFARE THIS IS LIKE A HOLIDAY.

THEN TERROR STRIKES! GUARDING A WELL-WORN PATH IS THE HUGE AND MENACING FIGURE OF A GIANT, OR IS IT A TROLL?
NEXT WEEK - The Mysterious Ruin

1305

2-11-62

Prince Valiant
IN THE DAYS OF KING ARTHUR
WRITTEN AND ILLUSTRATED BY HAROLD R FOSTER

Our Story: TERROR HOLDS THEM IN ITS GRIP. THEN, WITH TREMBLING HAND PRINCE VALIANT GUIDES HIS HORSE TOWARD THE TOWERING HORROR. FOR HE HAS REMEMBERED WISE MERLIN'S TEACHING; THAT THE SEEMINGLY WEIRD OR UNUSUAL GENERALLY HAS A LOGICAL EXPLANATION.

AS HE CAUTIOUSLY ADVANCES, VAL GAINS CONFIDENCE, FOR HIS HORSE SHOWS NO SIGN OF NERVOUSNESS, AS IT WOULD WERE THE FIGURE A LIVING THING.

PLASTER! BUT TURNED OUT BY THE HAND OF A MASTER CRAFTSMAN. VAL IS CURIOUS. WHAT LIES AHEAD ON THIS PATH THAT SUCH A GUARDIAN BE SET HERE TO SCARE AWAY INTRUDERS?

HE RIDES UP THE TRAIL AND COMES TO A WIDE VALLEY WHERE CULTIVATED FIELDS AND GARDENS RIPEN IN THE SUN AND FLOCKS OF SHEEP GRAZE ON THE HILLSIDE. THERE IS NO SIGN OF HOUSES OR WORKERS.

WHEN VAL RETURNS TO ARN AND JUSTIN HE IS THOUGHTFUL. *"THAT FIGURE IS TO FRIGHTEN INTRUDERS FROM THE PATH THAT LEADS UP TO FIELDS AND PASTURE, SO WE WILL FOLLOW IT DOWNWARD AND SEE WHAT IS AT THE OTHER END."*

HIGH ON A ROCKY SPUR STANDS A GUTTED AND FIRE-BLACKENED MONASTERY, GRIM EVIDENCE THAT THE VISIGOTHS HAVE PASSED THIS WAY.

BUT THE PATH ENDS ON A PLATEAU, WHILE THE STEPS LEADING TO THE CRUMBLING RUIN ARE WEED-GROWN FROM DISUSE.
NEXT WEEK- **The Fearful Cavern**

1306

2-18-62

Prince Valiant

IN THE DAYS OF KING ARTHUR

WRITTEN AND ILLUSTRATED BY HAROLD R FOSTER

Our Story: PRINCE VALIANT SITS DOWN TO PONDER A MYSTERY. A PATH LEADS FROM CULTIVATED FIELDS TO THIS PLATEAU.....AND ENDS. THE RUINS OF A FIRE-BLACKENED ABBEY LOOM ABOVE THEM, BUT HE CAN SEE NO SIGN OF ANY PEOPLE. JUSTIN PREPARES THE MIDDAY MEAL AND ARN SEARCHES FOR FIREWOOD.

A PILE OF BRUSHWOOD PROMISES A PLENTIFUL SUPPLY, BUT WHEN HE ATTEMPTS TO PULL SOME LOOSE, THE WHOLE MASS TOPPLES FORWARD REVEALING THE MOUTH OF A CAVE.

ARN SCREAMS WITH TERROR AS NIGHTMARE MONSTERS GLOWER AT HIM FROM THE DARKNESS.

EVEN VAL'S COURAGE MIGHT HAVE FAILED HIM HAD THEY NOT BEEN FRIGHTENED ONCE BEFORE THAT DAY BY A FIGURE OF PLASTER. THESE TOO ARE THE WORK OF MEN AND NOT FROM THE UNDER-WORLD.

"A MASTER SCULPTOR, MANY ASSISTANTS. FEAR IS THEIR DEFENSE, THEREFORE WEAK AT ARMS; THE TUNNEL LEADS UPWARD TOWARD THE ABBEY, SO WE WILL VISIT IT. BUT WE WILL NOT RISK THIS DARK WAY."

JUSTIN FOLLOWS CLOSE BEHIND VAL, SHAKING WITH FEAR, FOR TO HIS SUPERSTITIOUS MIND, EVEN THE PLASTER DEMONS HAVE THE POWER OF EVIL.

1307.

"PUT UP YOUR SWORDS," SAYS VAL. "I DO NOT DOUBT THAT WE ARE BEING WATCHED, SO SHOW THAT WE COME IN PEACE."

NEXT WEEK - **The Abbot**

HAL FOSTER

2-25-62

Prince Valiant
IN THE DAYS OF KING ARTHUR
WRITTEN AND ILLUSTRATED BY HAROLD R FOSTER

Our Story: PRINCE VALIANT, ARN AND JUSTIN CLIMB THE BROKEN, WEED-GROWN STAIRWAY TO THE GUTTED MONASTERY. THEY EXPECTED MORE HORRORS LIKE THOSE GRAVEN IMAGES THAT HAD SO FRIGHTENED THEM IN THE CAVERN.

THE NAVE OF THE ABBEY IS CHOKED WITH DEBRIS, BUT AT THE FAR END THE CHOIR AND ALTAR ARE INTACT, SWEPT CLEAN AND SHOWING SIGNS OF BEING WELL USED.

AS BECOMES A CHRISTIAN KNIGHT AND A FELLOW OF THE ROUND TABLE, VAL KNEELS BEFORE THE ALTAR TO REDEDICATE HIS SWORD TO THE SERVICE OF HIS KING AND HIS GOD.

A DOOR IN THE CHANCEL OPENS AND AN ABBOT APPEARS. "WE BID A MOST HEARTY WELCOME TO CHRISTIAN GENTLEMEN. IT IS SELDOM IN THESE WARLIKE DAYS THAT WE HAVE VISITORS WHO COME IN PEACE."

"WE HAVE LEFT THE ABBEY IN RUINS, SO PASSING WAR BANDS WILL THINK THE WHOLE MONASTERY ABANDONED AND LEAVE US IN PEACE," EXPLAINS THE ABBOT. "WE KEEP HIDDEN BEHIND OUR WALLS. ONLY THOSE WHO TILL OUR FIELDS LEAVE BY THE SECRET PASSAGE BEFORE DAWN AND RETURN AFTER DARK."

HAL FOSTER

BUT EVEN AS HE SPEAKS A WAR BAND IS LOOKING THEIR WAY. FOR A SCOUT HAD SEEN VAL AND HIS COMPANIONS ENTER THE ABBEY.
NEXT WEEK—The Warning Cry

1308.   3-4-62

Prince Valiant
IN THE DAYS OF KING ARTHUR
WRITTEN AND ILLUSTRATED BY HAROLD R FOSTER

Our Story: THE ABBOT HAD LIVED THROUGH THAT AWFUL DAY WHEN THE MONASTERY WAS SACKED AND BURNED, AND HE IS JUSTLY PROUD OF THE RESTORATION HE AND THE OTHER SURVIVORS HAVE ACCOMPLISHED.

"OUR ORDER SENDS SCHOLARS AND TEACHERS OUT INTO THE WORLD TO KEEP THE LAMPS OF LEARNING BRIGHT IN THIS DARK AGE. AMONG THESE BROTHERS ARE OUR MASONS, WEAVERS, COOKS, FARMERS AND OTHER CRAFTSMEN."

"AND THIS IS BROTHER JOHN, OUR SCULPTOR. HIS IMAGES OF SAINTS AND MARTYRS ADORN THE HIGH ALTAR AND HIS PLASTER DEMONS FRIGHTEN AWAY INTRUDERS."

"I KNOW," ANSWERS VAL, "FOR THEY ALMOST FRIGHTENED US WITLESS."

THE ABBOT IS AS HAPPY AS A SCHOOLBOY ON A HOLIDAY, FOR IT IS ALL TOO SELDOM THAT HE HAS A VISITOR TO WHOM HE CAN DISPLAY WHAT THE BROTHERS HAVE ACCOMPLISHED. THEN COMES THE CRY OF WARNING.

A SLENDER YOUTH IN RICH ATTIRE IS GALLOPING UP THE ROCKY PATH CRYING CHEERFULLY: "THE GOTHS ARE COMING!"

1309

THE WAR BAND EMERGES FROM THE DARK FOREST AND CLIMBS STEADILY UPWARD, THE SUN GLEAMING OFF A THOUSAND SPEAR POINTS.

"NOW, BROTHER JOHN, YOU HAVE A CHANCE TO UNVEIL YOUR MASTERPIECE. WE WILL ALL PRAY FOR YOUR SUCCESS, FOR THE LIVES OF OUR BROTHERS ARE AT STAKE."

NEXT WEEK- The Moment of Peril

3-11-62

Prince Valiant
IN THE DAYS OF KING ARTHUR
WRITTEN AND ILLUSTRATED BY HAROLD R FOSTER

Our Story : "THE GOTHS ARE COMING, PREPARE A WELCOME!" SHOUTS A YOUTH AS HE URGES HIS TIRED MOUNT UP THE STEEP PATH TO THE MONASTERY.

"PRINCE VALIANT, MEET STEPHAN, A WORLDLY YOUTH WHO SHOWS LITTLE SIGN OF REPENTANCE," SIGHS THE ABBOT, "BUT THANKS FOR THE TIMELY WARNING."

THE GOTHS FOLLOW, A THOUSAND STRONG. THEY HAVE SEEN MEN AMID THE RUINS OF THE ABBEY, AND WHERE THERE ARE MEN THERE IS LOOT OR, BETTER STILL, FOOD.

UNTIL THEY LEFT THEIR NORTHERN FORESTS THIS WARBAND HAD NEVER SEEN A BUILDING LARGER THAN A COTTAGE. NOW, AFTER TWO YEARS OF WANDERING ACROSS PLUNDERED GAUL, TALL BUILDINGS OF STONE MEAN FORTS OR CASTLES, HARD FIGHTING AND DEFEAT.

IN A CRYPT BELOW THE CHAPEL JUSTIN, WITH FLINT AND STRIKING IRON, SENDS A SPARK INTO A HEAP OF STRAW WHICH BROTHER JOHN BLOWS INTO A FLAME, AND THE SMOKE ASCENDS TO OPENINGS IN THE CEILING.

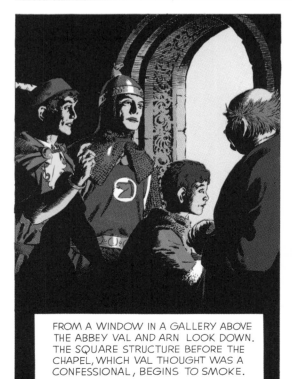

FROM A WINDOW IN A GALLERY ABOVE THE ABBEY VAL AND ARN LOOK DOWN. THE SQUARE STRUCTURE BEFORE THE CHAPEL, WHICH VAL THOUGHT WAS A CONFESSIONAL, BEGINS TO SMOKE.

THE PAGAN WARBAND CROWD THE ENTRANCE AND CLIMB THE HEAP OF DEBRIS. AWED BY THE SILENT EMPTINESS, THEY ADVANCE SLOWLY TO WHERE GOLD AND SILVER SHINE ON THE ALTAR. THEN A PUFF OF SMOKE HALTS THEM.

NEXT WEEK— **The Monster**

1310.　　　HAL FOSTER　　　3-18-62

Our Story: FROM A WINDOW HIGH IN THE GALLERY PRINCE VALIANT AND ARN LOOK DOWN AT THE PAGAN WARBAND AS THEY SURGE FORWARD. THEY ARE STRANGELY QUIET AS IF OVERAWED BY THE STILL, SILENT GRANDEUR OF THE RUINED ABBEY.

THEN A CLOUD OF SMOKE BELLOWS UP FROM THE WOODEN SCREEN, WHICH OPENS, SEALING OFF THE ALTAR. FOR A MOMENT THE WHOLE END OF THE BUILDING IS OBSCURED, AND THIS IS ENOUGH IN ITSELF TO BRING FEAR TO THE PRIMITIVE MINDS OF THE BARBARIANS.

A GASP OF HORROR RUNS THROUGH THE PAGAN THRONG AS A SHADOWY FORM APPEARS DIMLY IN THE SWIRLING CLOUD. THEN THE SMOKE THINS, REVEALING A MONSTER SO HUGE AND MENACING THAT PANIC AKIN TO MADNESS GRIPS THE WATCHERS AND, SCREAMING, THEY TRAMPLE EACH OTHER IN A WILD SCRAMBLE TO ESCAPE.

NEXT WEEK— **The Dancers**

3-25-61

Prince Valiant

IN THE DAYS OF KING ARTHUR

WRITTEN AND ILLUSTRATED BY HAROLD R FOSTER

Our Story: FROM OUT OF A CLOUD OF SMOKE (THAT SMELLS SUSPICIOUSLY LIKE WET STRAW BURNING) THERE APPEARS A TERRIBLE DRAGON, AND THE SAVAGE WAR-BAND FLEE IN SCREAMING TERROR.

THE GENTLE BROTHERS WATCH IN GLEE AS THE GOTHS GO LEAPING DOWN THE MOUNTAINSIDE, CARELESS OF BROKEN BONES AND LOST WEAPONS.

"NOW WE WILL REPAIR TO THE CHAPEL AND GIVE THANKS FOR OUR DELIVERANCE," ANNOUNCES THE ABBOT, "AND WE MUST COMMEND BROTHER JOHN ON HIS ARTISTRY."

BUT BROTHER JOHN IS ALREADY GIVING THANKS IN HIS OWN WAY. SINGING A CATCHY DITTY HE IS DANCING A JIG AROUND HIS PLASTER DRAGON.

"BROTHER JOHN, CEASE!", THUNDERS THE ABBOT. "YOUR UNSEEMLY LEVITY DOES NOT BECOME ONE OF OUR ORDER. WORLDLY PRIDE IS A SIN, SEEK GRACE IN THE PRACTICE OF HUMILITY!"

"OH, THESE ARTISTS!" COMPLAINS THE ABBOT, "THEY ARE ALL ALIKE; FRIVOLOUS, FULL OF VAINGLORY AND CONCEIT. THERE IS NO TRUE PENITENCE IN THEM!"

ALL THROUGH THE EVENING MEAL THE ABBOT SEEMS LOST IN THOUGHT. "NOW, HOW DID IT GO?" HE IS HEARD TO MUTTER AS HE WAVES HIS WOODEN SPOON.

BUT THAT NIGHT WHEN PRINCE VALIANT AND HIS SON PASS THE ENTRANCE TO HIS CELL, THEY HEAR HIM EXCLAIM: "AH, NOW I REMEMBER IT!" THEN THEY TIPTOE AWAY AND LEAVE THE ABBOT TO HIS LITTLE MOMENT OF WORLDLY JOY.
NEXT WEEK— The Gay Fugitive

1312.

4-1-62

Prince Valiant
IN THE DAYS OF KING ARTHUR

WRITTEN AND ILLUSTRATED BY HAROLD R FOSTER

Our Story: AT LAST COMES THE HOUR OF PARTING. PRINCE VALIANT AND ARN BID FAREWELL TO THE PEACEFUL BROTHERS AND LEAVE THE MONASTERY BY WAY OF THE SECRET TUNNEL. JUSTIN SHUDDERS AS HE PASSES THE AWFUL IMAGES THAT GUARD THE PASSAGEWAY.

JUSTIN LOOKS BACK. WAR, BRUTALITY, HUNGER AND PAIN ARE THE LOT OF THE MERCENARY SOLDIER. HOW HE LONGS FOR THE PEACE AND SERENITY HE IS LEAVING BEHIND.

STEPHAN LEADS THE WAY OVER THE FAINT GOAT TRAILS HE HAS KNOWN SINCE CHILDHOOD. "LOOK," HE EXCLAIMS, "THERE GOES THE GOTH WARBAND. THEY HAVE FOUND THE PASS AND ARE GOING OVER THE MOUNTAINS INTO HISPANIA, AND WE WILL BE WELL RID OF THEM."

THROUGH THE PASS ABOVE THE VILLAGE OF RONCESVALLES THE WARBAND WINDS LIKE A GLITTERING SERPENT. HERE, THREE CENTURIES LATER, THE MIGHTY CHARLEMAGNE WILL MEET WITH DEFEAT, AND ROLAND DIE A HERO'S DEATH.

ONE DAY THEY LOOK DOWN ON A WALLED CITY, ITS TOWERS AND BASTIONS AGLOW IN THE SUNSET. "THERE RULES SADONICK, DUKE OF AQUELOEN, ON THE DUCAL THRONE RIGHTLY MINE," SAYS STEPHAN.

1313.

"THE FALSE DUKE HAS MURDERED EVERY RELATIVE THAT MIGHT THREATEN HIS RULE. I, THE RIGHTFUL DUKE, HAVE BEEN A FUGITIVE FROM HIS ASSASSINS SINCE CHILDHOOD."

IN THE MORNING THEY PART, STEPHAN TO GO BY SECRET WAYS TO ONCE AGAIN SEE HIS MOTHER, AND VAL, DESPITE ALL WARNINGS, TO ENTER THE WALLED CITY.

NEXT WEEK—**The Duke**   4-8-62

Prince Valiant
IN THE DAYS OF KING ARTHUR
WRITTEN AND ILLUSTRATED BY HAROLD R FOSTER

Our Story: DESPITE STEPHAN'S WARNING, PRINCE VALIANT RIDES THROUGH THE CITY GATES OF DUKE SADONICK'S STRONGHOLD. FOR VAL CANNOT BELIEVE THAT THE DUKE COULD BE SO EVIL A RULER AS STEPHAN HAS DESCRIBED.

WHEN ONE NOBLE CROSSES THE DOMAIN OF ANOTHER, IT IS CUSTOMARY TO PAY THE RULING ONE A COURTESY CALL.

THE DUKE IS AT WORK, AND ARN'S EYES GROW BIG WITH HORROR. EXCEPT FOR A HARDENING OF HIS JAW, VAL'S EXPRESSION DOES NOT CHANGE . . . .

FOR THE DUKE IS SITTING AMONG A NEAT ARRAY OF GLEAMING INSTRUMENTS, AND BEFORE HIM, STRETCHED UPON THE RACK, IS THE LIMP FORM OF ONE OF HIS UNFORTUNATE ENEMIES.

DUKE SADONICK WIPES HIS HANDS ON A WHITE NAPKIN AND GREETS HIS GUESTS. "I CAN SEE YOU HAVE THE ARTISTIC TOUCH," COMPLIMENTS VAL. "AH, YES," ANSWERS THE DUKE MODESTLY, "I DO HAVE SOME TALENT, AND DISPLAYING IT THUS INSURES THE LOYALTY OF MY COURTIERS."

REFRESHMENTS ARE ORDERED AND VAL MUST ANSWER MANY SHREWD QUESTIONS.

1314.

THEY ARE SHOWN TO THEIR QUARTERS AND JUSTIN BRINGS IN THEIR SADDLEBAGS.
"GUARD YOUR TONGUES," VAL ORDERS. "THE DUKE HAS AN ARMY OF SPIES, OUR EVERY WORD IS REPORTED. HE EVEN KNOWS STEPHAN IS NEAR, AND WE KNOW THE DOOM IN STORE FOR HIM WERE HE TAKEN!"

NEXT WEEK—Bait for the Trap

4·15·62

Our Story: PRINCE VALIANT FINDS HIM-SELF THE GUEST OF DUKE SADONICK, AND HIS HOST HAS GREAT CHARM AND IS BRILLIANT IN CONVERSATION. IT IS HARD TO BELIEVE HIM THE SAME MAN WHO, ONLY YESTERDAY, TORTURED A VICTIM ON THE RACK.....

......UNTIL VAL DISAGREES WITH HIM ON SOME MINOR POINT. THEN HIS FACE HARDENS, HIS EYES GLITTER WITH RAGE, AND VAL IS GLAD WHEN THE MEETING IS OVER.

ONE THING IS CERTAIN. THE DUKE IS MAD WITH POWER AND WILL BROOK NO OPPOSITION TO HIS WILL, AND THERE IS ONLY ONE WHO STANDS IN HIS WAY... STEPHAN!

FEAR HAS TURNED EVERY COURTIER INTO AN INFORMER, EVERY SERVANT A SPY. ONLY IN THE SPACIOUS COURTYARD CAN THEY SPEAK TOGETHER WITHOUT BEING OVERHEARD. *"WE MAY HAVE TO LEAVE THIS MISCHANCY PLACE SUDDENLY,"* SAYS VAL, *"AND WE WILL NEED OUR MOUNTS OUTSIDE THE GATES."*

VAL'S VOICE IS RAISED IN ANGER SO ALL CAN HEAR; *"I TOLD YOU TO KEEP THE HORSES IN GOOD CONDITION, KNAVE. EXERCISE THEM! TWICE DAILY RUN THEM IN THE MEADOW BELOW THE CITY GATES."* JUSTIN MOUNTS SULLENLY AND RIDES OUT.

THE GATEKEEPERS BECOME USED TO THE COMING AND GOING OF JUSTIN AND PAY LITTLE ATTENTION TO HIM.

NOW THAT THEY HAVE STAYED THE NUMBER OF DAYS DEMANDED BY COURTESY, VAL AND ARN BID THE DUKE FAREWELL.

"BUT NO, SIR VALIANT, I HAVE NEED OF YOU AND THE YOUNG PRINCE TO BAIT A TRAP FOR STEPHAN. YOU RECOGNIZE THE NECESSITY, I HOPE, FOR STEPHAN STANDS IN MY WAY."

NEXT WEEK- **The Hostage**

HAL FOSTER

1315.

4-22-62

Our Story: THE DUKE IS SMILING AS HE INFORMS PRINCE VALIANT: "ONLY STEPHAN STANDS IN MY WAY. HE IS NOW VISITING HIS MOTHER'S FORTRESS CASTLE. YOU ARE TO GO TO HIM AND, AS A TRUSTED FRIEND, DECOY HIM OUT INTO OUR AMBUSH."

"AND TO INSURE THAT YOU WILL OBEY OUR WILL FAITHFULLY, YOUR SON ARN WILL BE CHAINED BESIDE THE RACK UNTIL YOU RETURN."

VAL STRIVES TO FORM PLANS OF ESCAPE, ONLY TO ABANDON EACH IN TURN. FINALLY IN DESPERATION HE WHISPERS TO JUSTIN: "FIND THE WAY TO STEPHAN AND WHEN NEXT YOU EXERCISE THE HORSES BEYOND THE GATES, RIDE TO HIM WITH A WARNING!"

SO JUSTIN DECAMPS WITH THE THREE HORSES. AND HE SPEEDS BACK ALONG THE WAY THEY HAD COME UNTIL HE REACHES THE SPOT WHERE THEY PARTED FROM STEPHAN. THEN HE FOLLOWS THE GOAT TRACK STEPHAN HAD TAKEN ALONG THE MOUNTAIN SIDE.

IT IS A FULL DAY BEFORE VAL DISCOVERS THAT HIS FALSE SQUIRE HAS STOLEN ALL THEIR HORSES, AND HIS ANGER SEEMS ALMOST REAL AS HE OFFERS A RICH REWARD FOR HIS CAPTURE.

BUT THE DUKE IS SUSPICIOUS: "COULD YOU HAVE SENT HIM TO WARN STEPHAN?" HE ASKS. "WELL, HARDLY!" GRUMBLES VAL, "FOR THE KNAVE TOOK ALL OUR MOUNTS, OUR ONLY MEANS OF ESCAPE."

1316.

VAL IS SAVED FROM FURTHER QUESTIONING BY THE ARRIVAL OF THE CHAMBERLAIN, AND THE WHISPERED MESSAGE HE BRINGS CAUSES THE DUKE TO SMILE EVILLY.

NEXT WEEK- A Time of Terror

4-29-62

Our Story : IN THE TOWN OF AQUELOEN DUKE SADONICK RULES BY SHEER TERROR, AND DEATH COMES MOST HORRIBLY TO THOSE WHO CROSS HIS WILL. ONLY HIS NEPHEW, STEPHAN, STANDS BETWEEN HIM AND ABSOLUTE RULE.

AND THE DUKE HAS CHOSEN PRINCE VALIANT TO BETRAY STEPHAN TO HIS DEATH. ARN IS TO BE HELD AS A HOSTAGE TO ASSURE THE AWFUL DEED IS DONE.

IT FALLS TO JUSTIN'S LOT TO CARRY VAL'S WARNING TO STEPHAN. WELL HE KNOWS THAT THE DUKE HAS SPIES EVERYWHERE, SO HE LEAVES THE HORSES WITH A SHEPHERD AND BORROWS HIS SMOCK.

IT WOULD BE IMPOSSIBLE FOR A HUMBLE SHEPHERD TO GAIN AUDIENCE WITH A NOBLEMAN, BUT JUSTIN IS IN LUCK. HE MEETS STEPHAN AS HE RIDES A-HAWKING.

"THE DUKE PROMISED DEATH ON THE RACK FOR YOUNG ARN UNLESS PRINCE VALIANT AGREED TO BETRAY YOU INTO HIS EVIL HANDS." STEPHAN IS THOUGHTFUL. "THIS IS TERRIBLE," HE SAYS, "FOR THE DUKE IS LIKE A MAD DOG AND WILL KILL ALL WHO FAIL HIS COMMANDS."

"HE WILL NOT TRY TO STORM THE CASTLE. HE HAS TRIED AND FAILED; IT IS ONLY BY TREACHERY..... TREACHERY! WHY CANNOT WE TRY TREACHERY, TOO?"

"MOTHER, GET READY TO GO WITH ME TO OUR HUNTING LODGE. WE WILL TAKE A FEW FRIENDS AND SERVANTS AND STAY FOR A WEEK."

AND THIS IS THE NEWS A SPY BRINGS TO THE DUKE AND CAUSES HIM TO SMILE HIS EVIL, TRIUMPHANT SMILE.

NEXT WEEK - **A-Hunting we will go!**

5-6-62

Prince Valiant
IN THE DAYS OF KING ARTHUR
WRITTEN AND ILLUSTRATED BY HAROLD R FOSTER

Our Story : SOLDIERS GATHER BELOW THE CITY'S WALLS. TO PRINCE VALIANT'S PRACTICED EYE THE TROOP IS NOT LARGE ENOUGH FOR AN ASSAULT, SO THE DUKE MUST BE PLANNING FOR A RAID OR AMBUSH.

HE IS NOT LONG IN FINDING OUT. "WE RIDE AT DAWN," SAYS THE DUKE WITH A CRUEL SMILE, "AND YOU MAY FULFILL YOUR TASK WITHOUT STAIN TO YOUR HONOR. MEANWHILE, YOUR SON WILL BE CHAINED BESIDE THE RACK TO INSURE YOUR OBEDIENCE."

AT DAWN DUKE SADONICK LEADS FORTH HIS PICKED TROOP, AND VAL, IN HOPELESS RAGE, RIDES WITH HIM. A QUICK SWORD STROKE WOULD FINISH THE DUKE, BUT IT WOULD ALSO BRING ABOUT HIS SON'S DEATH BY TORTURE.

AND AT THE SAME HOUR STEPHAN AND HIS MOTHER ARE RIDING TO THEIR HUNTING LODGE. "YOU ARE JUST LIKE YOUR LATE FATHER," SHE SCOLDS, "ALWAYS THINKING OF SPORT. WHY DID YOU NOT STAY IN THE MON- ASTERY WHERE YOU WERE SAFE FROM YOUR UNCLE ?"

"UNCLE SADONDICK IS A VERY TREACH- EROUS MAN, BUT," HE ADDS PIOUSLY, "I DO HOPE NOTHING BAD HAPPENS TO HIM." THEN HE CHUCKLES.

1318.

THE HUNTING PARTY IS SETTLED COM- FORTABLY FOR THE NIGHT AND, HAD IT NOT BEEN FOR HIS MOTHER'S STEADY PRATTLE, HE MIGHT HAVE HEARD.....

.....THE BUSHES RUSTLING AS A HUNDRED ARMED MEN SURROUND THE QUIET HUNTING LODGE.

NEXT WEEK- **The Reluctant Sword**

5-13-62

Our Story: STEPHAN AND HIS MOTHER LOOK UP AS THE DOOR OPENS AND THERE IN THE FLICKERING CANDLELIGHT STANDS DUKE SADONICK, HIS CRUEL FACE ALIGHT WITH TRIUMPH.

FOLLOWED BY A DOZEN ARMED BULLIES, HE SEATS HIMSELF. *"YOU HAVE AVOIDED ME ALL THESE YEARS, STEPHAN; NOW MY TURN HAS COME. SIR VALIANT! RID ME OF MY TROUBLESOME NEPHEW!"*

AS VAL HESITATES, THE DUKE'S FACE BECOMES DARK WITH ANGER. *"YOUR OWN SON AND HEIR STANDS CHAINED TO THE RACK. REFUSE MY BIDDING AND YOU SIGN HIS DEATH WARRANT."*

TO SAVE ARN FROM A HORRIBLE DEATH HE MUST DO A DEED THAT WILL BLIGHT HIS HONOR AND SCAR HIS VERY SOUL. HE DRAWS THE 'SINGING SWORD' AND IT COMES MOANING FROM ITS SCABBARD AND HANGS LEADEN IN HIS HAND, A LIFELESS THING.

THEN VAL STEPS IN FRONT OF STEPHAN AND FACES THE DUKE. HIS FACE RESOLUTE, THE LUST FOR BATTLE IN HIS EYES, HE STRIKES THE TABLE WITH THE GLITTERING BLADE AND ONCE MORE IT SINGS, EAGER, TRIUMPHANT!

"GUARDS! KILL THEM, KILL THEM ALL!" SCREAMS THE DUKE. AS THE GUARDS HESITATE BEFORE THE BRIGHT MENACE OF THE SWORD, A TRUMPET SOUNDS.

THE SILENCE OF THE NIGHT IS SHATTERED BY ANGRY SHOUTS AND THE CLASH OF ARMS. STEPHAN POINTS TO THE DOOR. *"MY MEN WERE IN THE FOREST AWAITING YOUR EXPECTED ARRIVAL, DEAR UNCLE, SO THE TRICKSTER HAS BEEN TRICKED!"*

NEXT WEEK— **A Ride for Life**

5-20-62

Prince Valiant IN THE DAYS OF KING ARTHUR

WRITTEN AND ILLUSTRATED BY HAROLD R FOSTER

Our Story: SADONICK, FALSE DUKE OF AQUELOEN, SITS QUIETLY WHILE STEPHAN'S MEN DISARM HIS BODYGUARD AND LEAD THEM AWAY. AND ALL THIS TIME STEPHAN'S MOTHER HAS GONE CALMLY ON WITH HER EMBROIDERY, BUT NOW HER PATIENCE IS AT AN END.

"SADONICK, YOU ARE AN INFERNAL NUISANCE, WHAT WITH ALL YOUR NOISE AND BLUSTER- ING YOU HAVE MADE ME BOTCH MY SEWING. STEPHAN, TAKE HIM OUT AND CUT OFF HIS HEAD, PLEASE."

SO MERCIFUL AN END WOULD NOT BE HIS. THE AWFUL CRUELTIES HE HAD INFLICTED WOULD CRY FOR VENGEANCE, A MORE LINGERING VENGEANCE.

PRINCE VALIANT SEES THE FURTIVE LOOK AS HE STEALTHILY TAKES A VIAL FROM HIS POUCH AND REMOVES THE STOPPER. THEN THE 'SINGING SWORD' FLASHES OUT.

"AN EASY DEATH BY POISON IS NOT FOR YOU. YOU ORDERED MY SON CHAINED TO THE RACK AS HOSTAGE FOR MY OBEDIENCE. SHOULD ANY HARM COME TO HIM, YOU WILL DIE ON YOUR OWN RACK!"

THEN HE MOUNTS AND RACES THROUGH THE NIGHT IN FRANTIC HASTE TO REACH AQUELOEN BEFORE NEWS OF THE DUKE'S CAPTURE ARRIVES.

AT DAWN A SPENT HORSE AND WEARY RIDER PASS THROUGH THE CITY GATES. ARE THEY TOO LATE?

1320.

VAL TOSSES THE REINS TO THE DIRTY- FACED STABLE BOY AND STRIDES INTO THE CASTLE TO FIND AN ANSWER TO HIS FEARS.
NEXT WEEK- **'Dirty Face'**

5-27-62

Prince Valiant
IN THE DAYS OF KING ARTHUR
WRITTEN AND ILLUSTRATED BY HAROLD R FOSTER

Our Story: WITH THE DAWN COMES PRINCE VALIANT BORN ON WINGS OF ANXIETY. STRAIGHT FOR THE DUKE'S CHAMBER OF HORRORS HE RACES. WILL HE FIND HIS SON ALREADY SUFFERING UPON THE RACK?

BUT THE CHAMBER IS EMPTY SAVE FOR THE DUKE'S ASSISTANT TORMENTORS, WHO COWER IN A CORNER.

"WE COULD NOT FIND YOUR SON. WE DID NOT CARRY OUT OUR MASTER'S ORDERS. SAVE US, SIR, OR WE MUST FACE THE DUKE'S ANGER!"

HE BIDS A TRUMPETER SOUND THE CALL AND WHEN ALL HAVE GATHERED IN THE HALL: "FIND MY SON, PRINCE ARN!" HE COMMANDS. "SEARCH EVERY CORNER OF THE CASTLE AND TOWN!" THEN, WHEN THEY HESITATE, ANNOUNCES: "SADONICK NO LONGER RULES HERE, HE IS IN THE HANDS OF STEPHAN, THE REAL DUKE."

VAL REMEMBERS THE MOUNT THAT HAD CARRIED HIM SO NOBLY THROUGH THE NIGHT. THE DIRTY-FACED STABLE BOY IS CARING FOR IT TENDERLY; "NOW, WHO WOULD RIDE A HORSE INTO THIS CONDITION?" HE ASKS THE ANIMAL. "I'D LIKE TO GIVE HIM RIDING LESSONS."

THE FAMILIAR VOICE, THE IMPUDENCE! VAL FIGHTS TO CONTROL HIS EMOTIONS. AT LAST HE TURNS SLOWLY......

...."YOUR FACE IS DIRTIER THAN USUAL," HE SAYS STERNLY, "GO GET READY FOR BREAKFAST. WASH YOUR NECK AND DON'T FORGET YOUR EARS!"

1321.

HAL FOSTER

ARN GOES OFF WHISTLING, AND WITH THE WEIGHT OF DESPAIR LIFTED, VAL LAUGHS AND WEEPS UNASHAMEDLY.

NEXT WEEK—A Wall Decoration

6-3-62

Prince Valiant
IN THE DAYS OF KING ARTHUR
WRITTEN AND ILLUSTRATED BY HAROLD R FOSTER

Our Story: IN THE CITY OF AQUELOEN ALL THE BELLS ARE RINGING, FLAGS WAVING, AS STEPHAN, THE REAL DUKE, COMES HOME. PRINCE VALIANT IS HONORED, FOR HE HAD FACED A TERRIBLE ORDEAL -- TO HOLD FAST TO HIS OATH, HIS HONOR AND HIS IDEALS AT THE RISK OF HIS SON'S LIFE.

MANY NOBLES WHO HAD SUPPORTED SADONICK WHEN HE USURPED THE DUCAL THRONE GATHER WHAT WEALTH THEY CAN ON SUCH SHORT NOTICE AND DEPART FOR LONG VACATIONS IN DISTANT LANDS.

THEN COMES THE PROBLEM OF DISPOSING OF SADONICK. BUT STEPHAN'S MATTER-OF-FACT MOTHER HAS ALREADY SOLVED THE PROBLEM. *"THE DECORATION YOU SEE OVER THE MAIN GATE IS HIS HEAD, A WARNING TO EVILDOERS. THE REST OF HIM WILL BE BURIED WITH FULL HONORS AS BEFITS ONE OF NOBLE BLOOD."*

A FEW MINOR OFFICIALS ARE EXECUTED IN THE MARKET PLACE TO SATISFY THE POPULAR DEMAND FOR ENTERTAINMENT; THEN STEPHAN'S RULE SETTLES DOWN INTO ROUTINE.

IT IS ABOUT THREE DAYS RIDE TO THE COAST WHERE ALETA SHOULD BE WAITING, BUT JUSTIN ASKS PERMISSION TO TURN BACK.

"AS A MERCENARY I HAVE KNOWN TWO YEARS OF BRUTALITY, HUNGER AND PAIN. I LONG FOR THE PEACE AND SERENITY OF LIFE IN THE MONASTERY WHERE WE FOUND STEPHAN."

1322

HAL FOSTER

THAT IS HOW BROTHER JOHN GOT AN ASSISTANT TO HELP HIM WITH THE HORRIBLE DEMONS THAT GUARD THE MONASTERY AND ITS GENTLE BROTHERS FROM PAGAN BANDS.

NEXT WEEK-**Heads You Lose**   6-10-62

Prince Valiant
IN THE DAYS OF KING ARTHUR
WRITTEN AND ILLUSTRATED BY HAROLD R. FOSTER

Our Story: THE SUNLIT STREETS OF AQUELOEN ECHO TO THE SOUNDS OF MERRIMENT, FOR THE TERRIBLE RULE OF THE FALSE DUKE SADONICK IS AT AN END AND HIS FUNERAL IS BEING CELEBRATED. HE IS BURIED IN TWO PIECES, FOR DURING HIS TRIAL HIS HEAD HAD BECOME SEPARATED FROM HIS SHOULDERS.

AT LONG LAST STEPHAN TAKES HIS RIGHTFUL PLACE ON THE DUCAL THRONE. THE CHRONICLES OF HIS TIME SHOW HIM TO BE A VERY POOR RULER, SPENDING ALL HIS TIME IN HUNTING AND FROLIC.

BUT EVEN HIS MISMANAGEMENT WAS SO MUCH BETTER THAN THE HARSH RULE OF HIS LATE UNCLE THAT HIS NAME WENT DOWN IN HISTORY AS 'STEPHAN THE GOOD.'

ONE BY ONE THE LOYAL NOBLES RETURN FROM EXILE, AND THE TRAITORS BECOME SO FEW THAT THE HEADSMAN IS ABLE TO WIPE OFF HIS AXE AND RETURN TO HIS BAKERY SHOP. THEN PRINCE VALIANT AND ARN BID FAREWELL TO STEPHAN.

VAL AND ARN CONTINUE ON THEIR WAY. SOMETIMES THEY SPEND THE NIGHT WRAPPED IN THEIR CLOAKS ON A BED OF BOUGHS; OTHER TIMES THEY ARE FORTUNATE TO HAVE A ROOF OVER THEIR HEADS.

ALL DAY VAL HAS BEEN TESTING THE WEST WIND. "WHAT DO YOU SMELL, SIRE? I HOPE IT IS A HAUNCH OF ROAST VENISON." "THE SEA," ANSWERS HIS FATHER, "I SMELL THE SEA!"

THE SEA AT LAST! THEY HAVE CROSSED FROM THE MEDITERRANEAN SEA TO THE OCEAN, BUT HAVE FOUND NO SAFE ROAD FOR COMMERCE. SOMEWHERE ALONG THE SHORE ALETA IS WAITING. ARN LOOKS AT HIS ADORED HERO AND COMPANION WITH DISGUST. THERE IS A FATUOUS LOOK ON HIS FACE. "ALETA," HE CAROLS, "ALETA, ALETA!" "MUSH," MUTTERS ARN, AS HE GOES INTO A SULK.

NEXT WEEK— **Mr. Whiskers**

1523.   6-17-62

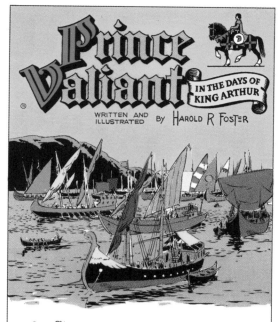

Prince Valiant

IN THE DAYS OF KING ARTHUR

WRITTEN AND ILLUSTRATED BY HAROLD R FOSTER

Our Story: AFTER SHE LEFT PRINCE VALIANT, ALETA HAD SAILED HER FLEET OF SHIPS AROUND SPAIN AND COME TO ANCHOR IN A SHELTERED COVE IN THE BAY OF BISCAY, THERE TO AWAIT THE ARRIVAL OF VAL AND ARN.

ALETA, AN ISLAND GIRL, HAD LEARNED TO SWIM EVEN AS SHE LEARNED TO WALK. SO IT IS NOT SURPRISING THAT HER OWN BROOD BECOME WATER-BABIES.

THEN COMES HER HOUR OF FREEDOM, TO SWIM AT RANDOM OR DIVE TO GLIDE AMONG THE WAVING SEAWEED. WATCHING HER, ONE CAN READILY BELIEVE THE LEGEND THAT SHE IS THE DESCENDANT OF A MERMAID.

AN OTTER IS THE PLAYBOY OF THE ANIMAL WORLD. HE MAKES SPORT OF EVERYTHING, AND TO FIND SOMEONE TO PLAY WITH IS JOY SUPREME.

WHERE SURF AND SAND MEET THEY COME TO REST, AND HERE HIS SENSITIVE BLACK NOSE TELLS HIM ALL ABOUT HIS NEW PLAYMATE; A FRIENDLY HUMAN, DELICIOUSLY WET AND UNAFRAID.

HE WHISTLES AND CHATTERS AN INVITATION TO COME PLAY SOME MORE AND SHE WHISTLES AND CHATTERS RIGHT BACK AT HIM. THEN HE SEES IT.....

.....ALL HIS LIFE HE HAS PLAYED WITH ROUND PEBBLES OR COLORED SHELLS, BUT THIS TOY SPARKLES AND GLEAMS AN INVITATION TO BE PUT TO SOME GOOD USE.

1324

HAL FOSTER

HIS POWERFUL JAWS SNIP THE JEWEL FROM ITS MOUNTING, AND WITH A SQUEAL OF DELIGHT, HE DIVES INTO THE WAVES, ALETA AFTER HIM. A CHASE, THIS WILL BE FUN!

NEXT WEEK- A Rival

6-24-62

Prince Valiant
IN THE DAYS OF KING ARTHUR
WRITTEN AND ILLUSTRATED BY HAROLD R FOSTER

Our Story: PRINCE VALIANT AND ARN COME AT LAST TO THE SEA AND BEHOLD ALETA'S WAITING FLEET. AS THEY RIDE FULL GALLOP TOWARD THE LANDING PLACE VAL'S EYE CATCHES SIGHT OF A FAMILIAR SPOT OF GOLD AMID THE BLUE WAVES.

LEAPING FROM HIS HORSE VAL RACES TOWARD THE BEACH, SHEDDING ARMS, ARMOR AND CLOTHING AS HE GOES.

WHENEVER ALETA GOES FOR A SWIM MR. WHISKERS, THE OTTER, WOULD RETRIEVE THE PURLOINED GEM FROM ITS HIDING PLACE, TEASE HER WITH IT, AND SHE WOULD CHASE HIM. OH, WHAT FUN!

THEN THE INTRUDER COMES. HE DOES NOT GLIDE SWIFTLY THROUGH THE WATER LIKE HIS PLAYMATE, BUT SURGES AHEAD USING BIG MUSCLES. MR. WHISKERS DOES NOT LIKE HIM.

HE CHATTERS A BIT AND ROLLS THE PLAYTHING IN HIS PAWS TO ATTRACT HER ATTENTION. NO USE, SHE DOES NOT WANT TO PLAY ANY MORE.... AT LEAST NOT WITH HIM.

HE FOLLOWS THEM UP THE BEACH IN A LAST DESPERATE ATTEMPT TO SAVE HIS FAIR COMPANION FROM A DULL, DRY LIFE, BUT TO NO AVAIL.

SO HE BITES HIS BIG, MUSCULAR RIVAL ON THE LEG AND RETURNS TO THE SEA.

HE TAKES THE GLEAMING TOY TO THE GROTTO WHERE HE KEEPS IT. SOMEHOW IT IS NOT MUCH FUN ANY MORE.

NEXT WEEK— **Farewell and Hello**

Prince Valiant
IN THE DAYS OF KING ARTHUR
WRITTEN AND ILLUSTRATED BY Harold R Foster

Our Story: ONCE AGAIN PRINCE VALIANT RETURNS AND IS QUICKLY REDUCED FROM A FAMED WARRIOR PRINCE TO A PLAIN HUSBAND AND FATHER. BUT HE IS CONTENT.

WHILE SHE BINDS UP HIS BITTEN LEG ALETA EXPLAINS ABOUT HER PLAYMATE AND THE STOLEN JEWEL.

A LONELY FIGURE WATCHES FROM THE BEACH AS THE FLEET SAILS AWAY TAKING HIS PET HUMAN WITH IT.

WOMEN ARE NOTORIOUSLY FICKLE (SO SAY MEN) SO IT IS NO WONDER ALETA FORGETS HER ERSTWHILE PLAYMATE AS SHE WATCHES HER HUSBAND RENEW ACQUAINTANCE WITH HIS CHILDREN AND LISTENS TO ARN'S ACCOUNT OF HIS ADVENTURES.

THE MALE ANIMAL IS NOT TOO DIFFERENT, FOR WHEN HE SEES ANOTHER OTTER SLIDING ON HER BELLY DOWN A CLAY BANK, MR. WHISKERS SQUEALS WITH DELIGHT AND JOINS THE FUN.

THEN HE REMEMBERS THE BRIGHT TOY HE HAD SO MUCH FUN WITH. FROM THE GROTTO WHERE HE HAD HIDDEN IT, HE RETRIEVES ALETA'S JEWEL, WORTH A QUEEN'S RANSOM.

HE GIVES IT TO HIS NEW-FOUND PLAYMATE AND SHE, LIKE ANY OTHER FEMALE, IS DELIGHTED WITH THE SPARKLING BAUBLE ...THEY LIVED HAPPILY EVER AFTER.

1326.

AND VAL AND ALETA? WELL, THEY LIVED TOGETHER MUCH AS MARRIED PEOPLE DO EVERYWHERE.

NEXT WEEK-The Reluctant Nursemaid

7-8-62

Prince Valiant IN THE DAYS OF KING ARTHUR

WRITTEN AND ILLUSTRATED BY HAROLD R FOSTER

Our Story : WITH A FAIR WIND ALETA'S FLEET ROUNDS THE TIP OF BRITTANY AND COMES TO ANCHOR IN A SHELTERED BAY. THEN THE CAPTAINS ARE CALLED TO COUNCIL AND THE GREAT TRADING ADVENTURE BEGINS. FOR SAFETY THEY WILL SAIL IN GROUPS OF THREE, AND THE GOODS OF THE EAST ARE TO BE BARTERED FOR TIN AND FURS, ORNAMENTS OF GOLD, COTTON, AMBER AND AMBERGRIS.

ALL GOES WELL UNTIL BOLTAR IS INFORMED THAT HE IS TO CONVOY TWO MERCHANTMEN TO THULE. *"BY THE HAMMER OF THOR!"* HE BELLOWS, *"BOLTAR, KING OF SEA ROVERS, NURSEMAID TO FOXY HUCKSTERS? NO!"*

PRINCE VALIANT AND QUEEN ALETA ARE OF ROYAL BIRTH, AUTO-CRATS BOTH, AND TO HAVE THEIR AUTHORITY DENIED IN PUBLIC IS ENOUGH TO JUSTIFY CENSURE .... BUT NOT THE UPROAR THAT FOLLOWS.

"BOLTAR, STOP YOUR BELLOWING, A HERD OF WALRUS MAKES LESS NOISE!" ALETA HAS TO SHOUT TO MAKE HERSELF HEARD. THEN, MORE GENTLY; *"YOU WILL NOT HAVE TO BE A NURSEMAID, THIS VESSEL WILL MAKE A THIRD, AND YOU MAY CONDUCT OUR ROYAL FAMILY SAFELY TO CAMELOT."*

1327.

HAL FOSTER

"SPLENDID WIFE YOU HAVE THERE, VAL. KNOWS BETTER THAN TO GIVE ORDERS TO MEN, WHAT? I WISH MY TILLICUM..." AT THE MENTION OF HIS WIFE'S NAME HE LOOKS OFF INTO THE DISTANCE. BOLTAR, THE LUSTY SEA ROVER, HAS BECOME HOMESICK!

NEXT WEEK - **The Voice**

7-15-62

Prince Valiant

IN THE DAYS OF KING ARTHUR

WRITTEN AND ILLUSTRATED BY Harold R. Foster

Our Story: BOLTAR'S HEART TURNS HOMEWARD, LONGING FOR HIS NATIVE HEATH. BUT FIRST HE MUST LAND PRINCE VALIANT AND HIS FAMILY ON THE SHORES OF BRITAIN.

WITH A FULL COMPLEMENT OF WARRIORS THE DRAGONSHIP MUST REPLENISH ITS SUPPLIES OFTEN. IT IS SUNDAY AND THE MONASTERY BELLS ARE RINGING AS THEY ENTER THE LITTLE PORT.

VAL AND ALETA CLIMB THE HILL AND ARE WELCOMED BY THE ABBOT. THEN THEY HEAR 'THE VOICE' CLEAR AND THRILLING AS A TRUMPET ON A FROSTY MORNING.

THE BROTHERS IN PROCESSION GO TO SERVICE CHANTING, BUT 'THE VOICE' DOMINATES ALL, FILLING THE HALLS AND CORRIDORS WITH ITS MUSICAL SOUND.

"WOJAN HAS FINISHED HIS TRAINING AND WOULD LIKE TO RETURN TO BRITAIN TO FULFILL HIS MISSION, AND THESE TWO SCHOLARS, HIS FRIENDS SLEATH AND DUSTAD, WOULD LIKE TO ACCOMPANY HIM. MAY THEY SAIL WITH YOU?" ASKS THE ABBOT.

VAL AGREES, FOR THERE IS SINCERITY AND SIMPLE HONESTY IN WOJAN'S FACE. THE TWO SCHOLARS MAKE LITTLE IMPRESSION AS THEY STAND HUMBLY BEHIND 'THE VOICE'.

1328.

DURING THE SHORT VOYAGE WOJAN PREACHES AND THE SCHOLARS STAND ON EACH SIDE PROMPTING HIM. THE VIKINGS CANNOT UNDERSTAND HIM BUT HIS RINGING VOICE BRINGS MEMORIES OF ANCIENT HERO SAGAS. AND SO IT IS THAT VAL, IN ALL INNOCENCE, BRINGS TO BRITAIN A FORCE THAT WILL ROCK THE KINGDOM.

NEXT WEEK- **Aruak**

HAL FOSTER

·7-22-62·

Our Story: THE LONG JOURNEY THAT HAD TAKEN THEM TO DISTANT SEAS AND STRANGE LANDS IS AT AN END. PRINCE VALIANT AND ALETA BID BOLTAR FAREWELL WITH SMILES THAT HIDE THE NEARNESS OF TEARS. FOR IN THESE PERILOUS TIMES EACH FAREWELL MIGHT BE THE LAST.

WOJAN REFUSES TO RIDE AND HUMBLY WALKS THE DUSTY ROAD TO CAMELOT HIS TWO FRIENDS, SLEATH AND DUSTAD, FREE AT LAST FROM THE RIGORS OF MONASTIC LIFE, ACCEPT ALL THAT IS OFFERED.

BACK IN CAMELOT ONCE MORE, THEIR FAMILIAR ROOMS AND THE NOISE AND BUSTLE OF COURT LIFE SEEM ALL THE MORE EXCITING AFTER THE LONG SEA VOYAGE.

THEN VAL IS SUMMONED BEFORE KING ARTHUR AND MUST TELL OF HIS FAILURE TO ESTABLISH A SAFE ROAD TO ROME. "ALL EUROPE IS IN TURMOIL AND THE BARBARIANS RAID UP TO THE VERY WALLS OF ROME!"

THE AUDIENCE OVER, VAL IS FREE TO VISIT THE STABLES, TO SEE HIS WAR HORSE, ARVAK. IN THE COURTYARD WOJAN IS PREACHING, BUT NOW A CROWD OF WORKERS AND SERVANTS HAVE LEFT THEIR WORK TO LISTEN TO HIS VOICE.

ARVAK HAS RETURNED TO HIS WILD STATE A MAN-KILLER, NO STALL COULD HOLD HIM.

IN THE PASTURE ARVAK IS MONARCH, NO STALLION DARE CHALLENGE HIS RULE. MANY OWNERS ARE CLAMORING FOR THEIR MOUNTS, BUT THE HOSTLERS DARE NOT FACE THE GREAT RED STALLION TO GET THEM.

NEXT WEEK - **Oat Cakes**

1329.   7-29-62

Prince Valiant
IN THE DAYS OF KING ARTHUR
WRITTEN AND ILLUSTRATED BY HAROLD R FOSTER

Our Story: TOO LONG HAS PRINCE VALIANT BEEN AWAY. HIS GREAT WAR HORSE, ARVAK, HAS AGAIN BECOME A MAN-KILLER. HE RULES THE PASTURE AS A MONARCH, AND EVEN THE BOLDEST KNIGHTS COMPLAIN THAT THEY CANNOT GET THEIR RIDING HORSES AWAY FROM HIM.

ARVAK'S LEGS ARE SCARRED FROM KICKING DOWN STALLS AND FENCES; HIS NECK AND SHOULDERS BEAR THE MARKS OF BATTLE WITH OTHER STALLIONS, BUT HE RAISES HIS HEAD AT VAL'S WHISTLE.

OF ALL ANIMALS THE HORSE AND THE DOG TAKE PRIDE IN SERVING MAN, BUT EACH HAS A MEMORY AND ARVAK REMEMBERS THE BRUTALITY OF HIS FIRST MAN......

....AND HOW THAT MAN HAD TRIED TO MAKE HIS WILL SUPREME BY BREAKING THE SPIRIT OF HIS HORSE. AND ON THAT AWFUL DAY HE HAD BROKEN LOOSE AND BECOME A MAN-KILLER.

ARVAK ALSO REMEMBERS HAPPIER DAYS UNDER A NEW MASTER WHEN, IN THE CRASH OF BATTLE, HE HAD GLORIED IN HIS STRENGTH. THERE WAS TRUST AND COMPANIONSHIP TOO IN THE JOUST AS MASTER AND MOUNT BECAME AS ONE.

ARVAK APPROACHES AND LOOKS AT ALETA EXPECTANTLY. IN A FLASH VAL REMEMBERS THE DRUID PRIESTESS. IT WAS A WOMAN WHO HAD FIRST SHOWN THE PROUD HORSE ANY KINDNESS. AND SHE HAD FED HIM OATCAKES!

IF A DRUID PRIESTESS COULD WIN HIS TRUST, WHY NOT ALETA? MEMORIES OF A BITTER PAST MUST BE ERASED, AND TRUST IN HIS MASTER RESTORED.

1330.   8-5-62

VAL IS SO INTENT ON REGAINING HIS GREAT WAR HORSE THAT HE DOES NOT NOTICE THAT NOW THE RINGING VOICE OF WOJAN HAS EMPTIED THE KITCHENS, THE STABLES AND THE ARMORY. EVEN THE KNIGHTS AND THEIR LADIES THRONG THE GALLERIES.

NEXT WEEK—**Pride**

Our Story: KING ARTHUR HAS TRIED TO BRING CHRISTIANITY TO BRITAIN WITH GENTLENESS AND LOGIC BACKED UP WITH THE SWORD. BUT NOW HE IS IN FAIR WAY OF STARVING BECAUSE OF THAT FAITH.

FOR THE KITCHENS, STABLES, ARMORY AND STOREHOUSES ARE EMPTIED AS ALL CROWD AROUND WOJAN TO HEAR HIM PREACH AND LISTEN TO THE THRILLING SOUND OF HIS CLARION VOICE.

VAL IS ABLE TO ENLIST THE HELP OF SEVERAL KNIGHTS, WHO ARE ONLY TOO WILLING TO AID IN THE TAMING OF THE GREAT RED STALLION, SO THEY CAN RECLAIM THEIR OWN HORSES FROM HIS DOMINATION.

THE CORRAL HAS AN ESCAPE WAY WHERE ONLY A MAN CAN SQUEEZE THROUGH, AND THERE STANDS ALETA, AN OATCAKE IN HER OUTSTRETCHED HAND. VAL, IN FULL ARMOR, WHISTLES THE FAMILIAR CALL.

AT THE SIGNAL THE KNIGHTS TROOP BY IN ALL THE PANOPLY OF WAR, LEATHER CREAKING, BITS AND SPURS JINGLING, TRUMPETS SOUNDING.

THE MEMORIES OF A BITTER PAST FADE, FOR THERE BEFORE HIM ARE ALL THE THINGS HE HOLDS MOST DEAR. A GENTLE WOMAN WITH OATCAKES, A COMPANION HE CAN OBEY WITH PRIDE, AND BROTHER WAR HORSES ON PARADE.

ONLY FOR AN INSTANT DOES ARVAK TREMBLE, FOR HE CAN FEEL THE FEAR IN THE HEARTS OF THE STABLE BOYS. BUT CALM, CONFIDENT VOICES REASSURE HIM.

FROM THAT VALHALLA WHERE ALL WAR HORSES GO, A HUNDRED ANCESTORS LOOK DOWN WITH PRIDE AS THEIR DESCENDANT TAKES HIS RIGHTFUL PLACE AT THE HEAD OF THE TROOP, NECK ARCHED AND HOOFS PRANCING LIKE A DANCER.

NEXT WEEK— **Famine**

1331.

8-12-62

Prince Valiant
IN THE DAYS OF KING ARTHUR

WRITTEN AND ILLUSTRATED BY HAROLD R FOSTER

Our Story: MANY A MARE STARES BROKEN-HEARTED AFTER ARVAK AS HE GIVES UP HIS OVERLORDSHIP OF THE HERD AND ONCE AGAIN BECOMES A PROUD WAR HORSE, PRANCING AT THE HEAD OF THE TROOP.

AFTER HIS WILD, FREE LIFE AS UNDISPUTED MONARCH OF THE HERD ARVAK IS IN NEED OF MUCH GROOMING. PRINCE VALIANT MUST ATTEND TO THIS HIMSELF, AS THERE ARE NO STABLE BOYS AROUND.

THE CHIEF BUTLER ANNOUNCES THAT DINNER IS DELAYED, FOR COOKS AND SERVANTS HAVE LEFT THEIR WORK TO LISTEN TO THE PREACHING OF WOJAN.

"SIR VALIANT, YOU ARE RESPONSIBLE FOR BRINGING WOJAN TO OUR COURT. TELL ME IF HE IS THE GREAT TEACHER, NAY, THE PROPHET HE IS SAID TO BE, OR A TROUBLE MAKER!"
"I WILL STAKE MY HONOR ON HIS HONESTY," ANSWERS VAL, "BUT I WILL TRY TO FIND OUT MORE ABOUT HIM."

GREAT CROWDS NOW GATHER TO HEAR WOJAN PREACH; SPELL-BOUND THEY LISTEN TO THE RINGING VOICE. THE MAN'S DEEP SINCERITY CARRIES BOTH CONVICTION AND MYSTERY. BUT WHAT DOES HE SAY? TAG ENDS OF SERMONS, QUOTATIONS FROM THE SCRIPTURES, SCRAPS FROM LATIN PRAYERS. ONLY WHEN HIS ADVISORS PROMPT HIM DOES HE MAKE SENSE --

"WE MUST ALL MAKE SACRIFICE, FOR THE WORD MUST GO FORTH TO THE ENDS OF THE EARTH! A CATHEDRAL MUST BE ERECTED AND CHURCHES BUILT AS FORTRESSES AGAINST PAGANISM!"

WOJAN LEAVES WITH THE TWO SCHOLARS, BUT SLEATH HANGS BACK AND, WHEN WOJAN HAS GONE WITHIN, DIRECTS SOME SERVANTS TO GO AMONG THE THRONG AND TAKE UP A COLLECTION FROM THOSE WHO WISH TO MAKE A 'SACRIFICE'.

ALL IS AS IT SHOULD BE; THE EVANGELIST IS NOT CONCERNED WITH MONEY MATTERS BUT LEAVES COLLECTIONS TO HIS ASSISTANTS. YET VAL IS UNEASY. WOJAN HAS THE POWER TO UPSET ALL CAMELOT..... WHAT IF THAT POWER WERE MISUSED?
NEXT WEEK- **The Interview**

1332.
8-19-62

Prince Valiant

IN THE DAYS OF KING ARTHUR

WRITTEN AND ILLUSTRATED By Harold R Foster

Our Story: PRINCE VALIANT SPENDS THE DAWN HOURS ON THE PRACTICE FIELD, FOR IT WILL TAKE CONSIDERABLE TRAINING TO BRING ARVAK BACK TO THAT FINE CO-OPERATION BETWEEN HORSE AND RIDER SO NECESSARY IN COMBAT.

WOJAN AND THE TWO SCHOLARS HAVE QUARTERS ABOVE THE STABLE, AND VAL IS REMINDED OF THE KING'S REQUEST.

SO HE PAYS A VISIT TO WOJAN. IT IS A STRANGE INTERVIEW, FOR THE SCHOLARS, SLEATH AND DUSTAD, GIVE ALL THE ANSWERS. ONE THING VAL LEARNS; THAT WOJAN HAS THE SIMPLE MIND OF A CHILD AND TRUSTS IN THE WISDOM OF HIS TWO ADVISORS.

BUT WHEN VAL MENTIONS THE COLLECTIONS WOJAN IS WROTH. "COLLECTIONS!", HE BELLOWS, "WHAT COLLECTIONS? OUR ORDER IS PLEDGED TO POVERTY, FOR MONEY IS EVIL."
"IT IS THE ROOT OF EVIL", ADMITS SLEATH, "BUT WE MUST FIGHT EVIL WITH EVIL. MANY CONVERTS WILL FOLLOW YOU AND MUST BE FED, YOUR CATHEDRAL BUILT, AND THIS MONEY IS A FREE GIFT!"

"I WOULD YOU HAD NOT BROUGHT WOJAN TO CAMELOT, SIR VALIANT. KNIGHTS, ARCHERS, SERVANTS AND SERFS NEGLECT THEIR DUTIES TO HEAR HIM PREACH."

RELIEF FROM THESE WORRIES COMES UNEXPECTEDLY. SLEATH AND DUSTAD APPEAR AND REQUEST THE KING FOR HORSES, A WAGON, SUPPLIES AND A CONTRIBUTION.
"OUR MASTER WILL GO FORTH TO PREACH AGAINST EVIL AND CARRY THE WORD TO THE PAGANS AS SOON AS WE ARE EQUIPPED."
THE KING READILY AGREES EVEN THOUGH THE REQUEST SMACKS OF BLACKMAIL.

NEXT WEEK - **The Exodus**

HAL FOSTER

8-26-62

Our Story: IT IS THE DAY OF WOJAN'S DEPARTURE FROM CAMELOT, AND KING ARTHUR AND PRINCE VALIANT LISTEN TO HIS FAREWELL SERMON, AND THE WORDS, SPOKEN IN HIS COMPELLING VOICE, FILL THEM WITH UNEASINESS.

"THERE IS BUT ONE KING WHOSE LAW YOU MUST OBEY. HE IS THE KING OF KINGS ON HIGH. ALL EARTHLY KINGS ARE DUST AND MUST RETURN TO THE DUST FROM WHICH THEY SPRANG!" POOR SIMPLE WOJAN DOES NOT KNOW HE IS UNDERMINING THE AUTHORITY OF THAT EARTHLY KING, ARTHUR.

THEN WOJAN PASSES THROUGH THE GATES, WALKING BARE-FOOT AS USUAL, BUT HIS TWO ADVISORS, THE SCHOLARS SLEATH AND DUSTAD, RIDE THE HORSES THE KING HAS GIVEN THEM.

AT FIRST A FEW ZEALOTS FOLLOW THEIR TEACHER, THEN OTHERS JOIN, AND STILL OTHERS UNTIL A CONTAGION SEIZES ALL CAMELOT. SERVANTS, HOSTLERS, SMITHS AND EVEN GUARDSMEN DROP THEIR TOOLS AND JOIN THE PROCESSION.

VAL AND THE KING LOOK AT EACH OTHER IN AMAZEMENT. THEY HAVE WITNESSED THE BIRTH OF ONE OF THOSE STRANGE RELIGIOUS FERVORS THAT MARK THE DARK AGES, BEGINNING WITH THE QUEST OF THE GRAIL AND ENDING IN THE CRUSADES.

"I HAVE TRIED TO BRING CHRISTIANITY TO OUR REALM WITH LAW AND ORDER, BUT HAVE NOT BEEN ABLE TO RAISE SUCH ENTHUSIASM. HAVE I FAILED?"

WOJAN'S SIMPLE HEART OVERFLOWS WITH JOY. HE LEADS A GREAT THRONG THAT GROWS LARGER AS PEASANTS LEAVE THEIR FIELDS TO JOIN THE RANKS. THERE IS NO DISCIPLINE AND ALL ARE GROWING HUNGRY.

NEXT WEEK- **The Growing Menace**

1354.   9-2-62

Our Story: BECAUSE PRINCE VALIANT IS ONE OF THE VERY FEW WHO CAN READ BOOKS, HAS TRAVELED WIDELY, AND WAS A PUPIL OF WISE MERLIN, HE STANDS HIGH IN KING ARTHUR'S COUNCIL.

"WHAT OF THIS WOJAN, SIR VALIANT? HE GATHERS A MULTITUDE TO HEAR HIM PREACH, AND THEREAFTER THEY DENY OUR AUTHORITY. DOES HE PREACH SEDITION?"

"NO, SIRE, HE IS HONEST AND CHILDLIKE, BUT HE TRUSTS HIS ADVISERS BECAUSE OF THEIR SUPERIOR LEARNING, AND THEY MAY PROMPT HIM TO SAY THINGS THAT HAVE A DOUBLE MEANING."

IT IS EVEN AS VAL SAYS. SLEATH AND DUSTAD ARE NOW WEALTHY WITH THE GIFTS AND CONTRIBUTIONS THAT POUR IN (AND WHICH THEY KEEP), AND LOOK DOWN ON WOJAN AS A TOOL TO THEIR PLANS. AND WOJAN, SO ELATED AT THE SUCCESS OF HIS CRUSADE, FAILS TO NOTICE THIS.

WOJAN'S COMPELLING VOICE THRILLS HIS LISTENERS AND HIS JUMBLED SERMONS ONLY CREATE MYSTERY. PEASANTS AND SERFS LEAVE HOME AND FIELD TO JOIN THE AIMLESS PILGRIMAGE, FOR IT IS RUMORED THAT THE MASTER WILL LEAD THEM TO ETERNAL BLISS.

BUT HUNGER KNOWS NO MORALITY AND, UNKNOWN TO WOJAN, THE PILGRIMS PLUNDER AND LAY WASTE TO THE LANDS OVER WHICH THEY WANDER.

THE KING HEARS OF THE GROWING MENACE. "THIS WOJAN HAS SUCH A HOLD ON THE IMAGINATION OF THE ZEALOTS WHO FOLLOW HIM THAT TO CURB HIM MIGHT START THAT MOST TERRIBLE OF THINGS, A HOLY WAR. AND WITH US ON THE WRONG SIDE!"
"SIRE," SAYS VAL QUIETLY, "I THINK I HAVE A SOLUTION!"
NEXT WEEK- **The Humble Abbot**

1335.

9-9-62

Prince Valiant
IN THE DAYS OF KING ARTHUR
WRITTEN AND ILLUSTRATED BY Harold R Foster

Our Story : PRINCE VALIANT ARISES AND ADDRESSES THE KING: "SIRE, THIS WOJAN IS REGARDED AS A SAINT BY HIS MULTITUDE OF FOLLOWERS. TO CURB HIM BY FORCE WOULD START A TERRIBLE HOLY WAR. YET HE MUST BE STOPPED, FOR WHERE-EVER HIS AIMLESS PILGRIMAGE WANDERS THE LAND IS LAID WASTE."

"MY LADY ALETA AND I VISITED A MONASTERY IN BRITTANY," VAL CONTINUES. "THE ABBOT WAS A HUMBLE, KINDLY MAN, AND HIS AUTHOR-ITY OVER THE BROTHERS WAS GREAT."

"IT WAS HE WHO ASKED ME TO BRING WOJAN TO BRITAIN. THE HABIT OF OBEDIENCE IS HARD TO BREAK. WOJAN MAY ACCEPT THE COUNSEL AND ADVICE OF HIS ABBOT."

AND SO IT IS THAT VAL BRINGS THE ABBOT OUT OF BRITTANY AND THEY FOLLOW THE TRAIL OF RUIN THAT MARKS THE PASSAGE OF THE PILGRIMS.

THEY ENTER A VILLAGE UNTOUCHED BY THE THIEVES AND BULLIES THAT FOLLOW ON THE FRINGE OF THE PILGRIMAGE FOR THE SAKE OF PLUNDER.

"WE PAID FOR OUR SAFETY," THE MAYOR SAYS. "DUSTAD AND SLEATH OFFERED TO LEAD THEIR FOLLOWERS AWAY FROM OUR VILLAGE. THE PRICE WAS HIGH, BUT WE HAD HEARD WHAT HAPPENED TO OTHER VILLAGES, SO WE PAID."

THE OLD ABBOT SHAKES HIS HEAD. SUCH VILLAINY HE CAN HARDLY IMAGINE.

NEXT WEEK—**Tribute**

HAL FOSTER

1336.

9-16-62

Prince Valiant
IN THE DAYS OF KING ARTHUR
WRITTEN AND ILLUSTRATED BY HAROLD R FOSTER

Our Story: AS PRINCE VALIANT AND THE ABBOT DRAW EVER CLOSER TO THE PILGRIM HOST THE FULL HORROR OF THEIR PASSING UNFOLDS. THE OLD, THE LAME AND THE SICK ARE LEFT BEHIND TO DIE IN A PLUNDERED LAND.

HUNGER AND SUFFERING CREATE FANATICS; FOOD CAN RESTORE REASON. VAL SENDS A MESSAGE TO THE KING REQUESTING A WAGON TRAIN OF PROVISIONS.

WOJAN KNOWS NOTHING OF THE MENACE HE HAS CREATED, FOR SLEATH AND DUSTAD SURROUND HIM WITH A WELL-FED GUARD. THEIR WEALTH IS MOUNTING AND SOON, WITH A MAN REGARDED AS A SAINT TO DO THEIR BIDDING, THEY WILL BE THE STRONGEST FORCE IN BRITAIN.

THE NEXT VILLAGE VAL AND THE ABBOT COME TO IS BEING PILLAGED AND BURNED IN WANTON DESTRUCTION. ITS PEOPLE HUDDLE IN THE CHURCH FOR PROTECTION.

THE HALF-NAKED RABBLE ARE NO MATCH FOR AN ARMORED KNIGHT WITH A FLASHING SWORD AND MOUNTED ON A GREAT RED WAR HORSE WHOSE FLAILING HOOFS SCATTER THEM IN FEAR.

AGAIN THE NAMES OF SLEATH AND DUSTAD COME UP. *"WE PAID THEM A GREAT SUM FOR PROTECTION, BUT WE HAVE BEEN BETRAYED."*
NEXT WEEK- **The Reckoning**

HAL FOSTER

1337.   9-23-62

Prince Valiant
IN THE DAYS OF KING ARTHUR

WRITTEN AND ILLUSTRATED BY HAROLD R FOSTER

Our Story: PRINCE VALIANT AND THE ABBOT HAVE SEEN MISERY, VIOLENCE AND BETRAYAL IN THE WAKE OF THE PILGRIM HORDE. NOW THE ODOR OF AN UNWASHED MULTITUDE BECOMES STRONGER AND, DESPITE THE DISCOMFORT, THE ABBOT URGES HIS MOUNT INTO A GALLOP.

A VAST CROWD SURROUNDS A KNOLL UPON WHICH WOJAN STANDS, AND HIS GLORIOUS VOICE HOLDS THEM SPELLBOUND AND SILENT. ALTHOUGH THEY ARE TOO FAR AWAY TO UNDERSTAND HIS WORDS, THERE CAN BE NO DOUBT OF HIS DEEP SINCERITY.

VAL AND THE ABBOT DISMOUNT AND MAKE THEIR WAY THROUGH THE HUNGRY RABBLE AND ENTER WOJAN'S PAVILION.

THIS IS THE GREAT TEST. WILL THE ABBOT STILL HOLD ANY AUTHORITY OVER HIS OLD PUPILS? WOJAN RISES AND HUMBLY KNEELS TO RECEIVE THE ABBOT'S BLESSING.

"MY SON, YOU HAVE DONE NOBLY," SAYS THE ABBOT KINDLY, " BUT NOW IT IS TIME TO BUILD YOUR CATHEDRAL WITH THE TREASURE YOU AND YOUR ADVISERS HAVE GATHERED."
"TREASURE!" ECHO'S WOJAN IN ASTONISHMENT. "WHAT TREASURE?"

1338.

VAL LOOKS AT SLEATH AND DUSTAD. THOUGH IT SEEMS THEIR GAME IS UP, THERE IS A CONFIDENT SNEER ON THEIR FACES AS IF THEY HAD LONG PREPARED FOR THIS AND HAD MADE THEIR PLANS.

NEXT WEEK - **The Treasure.**

9-30-62

Prince Valiant
IN THE DAYS OF KING ARTHUR
WRITTEN AND ILLUSTRATED BY HAROLD R FOSTER

Our Story: PRINCE VALIANT AND THE ABBOT AT LAST CATCH UP WITH THE VAST HORDE OF PILGRIMS, AND THE CRUEL HOAX IS REVEALED. WOJAN IS STUNNED.

"YOU, MY LEARNED AND RESPECTED FRIENDS, YOU HAVE USED OUR HOLY MISSION TO MAKE A PROFIT?" EXCLAIMS WOJAN, LOATH TO BELIEVE SUCH GREED

"YES, YOU STUPID FOOL," SNARLS SLEATH, "WE ARE NOW MEN OF GREAT WEALTH AND POWER, AND YOU WILL DO AS WE DIRECT!"

"YOU ARE BUT A CHILD WITH A VOICE. IT IS WE WHO PUT THE WORDS IN YOUR MOUTH. WE MADE YOU AND WE CAN BREAK YOU!"

SLEATH AND DUSTAD ARE SO USED TO TREATING WOJAN AS AN INNOCENT CHILD THAT THEY HAVE FORGOTTEN THAT HE IS ALSO A MAN, A STRONG AND ANGRY MAN.

"GUARDS! GUARDS!" SHRIEKS THE BATTERED SLEATH, AND THE GROUP OF WELL-FED AND PAID BULLIES THEY HAD ASSEMBLED TO KEEP WOJAN FROM LEARNING THE TRUE STATE OF AFFAIRS, COME RUNNING.

"GUARD THE WAGONS!" BELLOWS DUSTAD.
"THAT MUST BE WHERE THE TREASURE IS HIDDEN. COME, WOJAN, AND TRULY EARN THE PRICE OF YOUR CHURCH. AND A THOROUGHLY AROUSED WOJAN FOLLOWS VAL TO THE WAGONS.

NEXT WEEK- **The Fight for the Treasure**

1339.

10-7-62

Prince Valiant
IN THE DAYS OF KING ARTHUR
WRITTEN AND ILLUSTRATED BY HAROLD R. FOSTER

Our Story: PRINCE VALIANT WITH THE 'SINGING SWORD' STANDS BACK TO BACK WITH WOJAN AND HIS CUDGEL, AND VERY FEW OF THE HIRED BULLIES ARE BRAVE ENOUGH TO DO BATTLE. THE REST SWARM OVER THE WAGONS, CLAWING AT THE TREASURE CHESTS.

NOT UNTIL THEY MOUNT THE WAGONS DOES THE REAL BATTLE BEGIN, AND IT IS FIERCE, FOR GREED IS SOMETIMES A SUBSTITUTE FOR COURAGE.

THE STARVING PILGRIMS BECOME AWARE THAT THEIR BELOVED PROPHET IS BEING ATTACKED AND VIOLENCE SWEEPS THE MULTITUDE LIKE A GRASS FIRE. IN THE TUMULT NO ONE KNOWS WHO HIS FOE IS.

CLEAR AS A BUGLE NOTE ON A BATTLEFIELD THE VOICE OF WOJAN RINGS OUT. BUT NOW VAL IS HIS PROMPTER. *"PEACE! PEACE!"* HE CALLS, *"FOR OUR LONG SUFFERING IS OVER. BY THE GRACE OF OUR GOOD KING ARTHUR, FOOD FOR ALL IS ON ITS WAY!"*

IT IS THE ABBOT HIMSELF WHO TENDS TO WOJAN'S WOUNDS. *"FEAR NOT, MY SON, GOOD WILL YET COME FROM ALL THIS EVIL. EVEN NOW MY CLERK IS COUNTING THE TREASURE, AND YOUR CHURCH MAY BE BUILT."*

1340

FAR INTO THE NIGHT THE DELIGHTED ABBOT WORKS ON PLANS FOR THE CHURCH. BUT AS HIS CLERK COUNTS THE TREASURE, THE PROJECT GETS BIGGER; A CLOISTER IS ADDED, A MONASTERY, GARDENS, A HOSPITAL......
ONLY VAL IS UNEASY. DID HIS MESSAGE REACH THE KING? DID THE KING RESPOND? HOW LONG CAN THIS STARVING RABBLE BE HELD IN CHECK?

NEXT WEEK- **The Reward**   10-14-62

Our Story: WOJAN AND THE ABBOT LISTEN HAPPILY AS THE CLERK COUNTS THE TREASURE. SLEATH AND DUSTAD HAVE BEEN VERY ENTERPRISING CROOKS AND THE TREASURE IS GREAT. ONLY PRINCE VALIANT IS WORRIED. WILL THE KING SEND FOOD FOR THE STARVING PILGRIMS..... AND WHAT TO DO WITH THE TWO RASCALS?

THE CLERK SOLVES THE LAST PROBLEM. *"I WAS A MAN OF DUBIOUS MORALS, WISE IN THE WAYS OF THE WORLD, BEFORE I JOINED THE BROTHERHOOD. I CAN SOLVE THE PROBLEM OF SLEATH AND DUSTAD WITHOUT BOTHERING THE KING."*

THE TWO SCOUNDRELS ARE AWAITING THE KING'S JUSTICE; THE CERTAINTY THAT THEY WILL SOON DECORATE THE GALLOWS HAS SERIOUSLY INTERFERED WITH THEIR PLANS FOR A LIFE OF EASE.

"YOU, SLEATH AND DUSTAD, ARE FREE TO GO," SAYS THE WILY CLERK. *"THOUGH YOUR METHODS WERE DISHONEST YOU HAVE MADE WOJAN'S CHURCH AND MONASTERY POSSIBLE. HERE IS YOUR REWARD. NOW GO!"*

WITH GREEDY EYES THEY EXAMINE THEIR REWARD: TWO WINE CUPS OF SOLID GOLD INLAID WITH AMETHYST. THEY ALSO BECOME AWARE OF OTHER GREEDY EYES. THEIR RUFFIAN BODYGUARD HAS GATHERED AROUND THEM.

THE PRECIOUS GOBLETS MIGHT HAVE MADE SLEATH AND DUSTAD COMFORTABLY RICH, BUT, AS THEY WERE NEVER HEARD OF AGAIN, WHO KNOWS?

THE CLERK RETURNS WITH GOOD NEWS. *"A MESSAGE HAS COME SAYING THAT A WAGON TRAIN OF PROVISIONS IS BUT A LEAGUE AWAY, AND"*... WITH A PIOUS SMIRK: *"I REWARDED OUR TWO BENEFACTORS. THEY ARE GREEDY MEN AND, ALAS, ARE FOLLOWED BY OTHER GREEDY MEN."*

NEXT WEEK- **Succor**

1341.

HAL FOSTER

10-21-62

Prince Valiant
IN THE DAYS OF KING ARTHUR
WRITTEN AND ILLUSTRATED BY HAROLD R FOSTER

Our Story: THE PROVISION WAGONS ARRIVE AND THE STARVING PIL-GRIMS ARE WILD WITH JOY. IT IS FORTUNATE THAT THE KING ALSO SENT A STRONG GUARD, ELSE THERE WOULD HAVE BEEN A FOOD RIOT WITH SOME GETTING TOO MUCH, OTHERS NOTHING.

PRAYERS ARE SAID FOR THEIR DELIVER-ANCE FROM STARVATION BY THE BOUNTY OF KING ARTHUR.

WOJAN SPEAKS: "HERE ON THIS KNOLL OUR CHURCH WILL RISE. ALL WHO ARE SKILLED WITH TOOLS, ALL WHO WISH TO LABOR MAY STAY AND, PERHAPS, JOIN OUR BROTHERHOOD. ON THE MORROW WAGONS OF PROVISIONS WILL RETRACE OUR ROUTE SO THOSE WHO WOULD RETURN TO THEIR HOMES MAY REACH THERE SAFELY."

PRINCE VALIANT LINGERS ON, CARRIED AWAY WITH ENTHUSIASM FOR THE BUILDING OF THE NEW CHURCH.

THE KING IS GENEROUS, SENDING ARCHITECTS, MASTER MASONS AND PROVISIONS TO AID VAL. THE END OF THE AIMLESS, DESTRUCTIVE PILGRIMAGE HAS RELIEVED HIM OF ONE MORE OF HIS WORRIES.
1342.

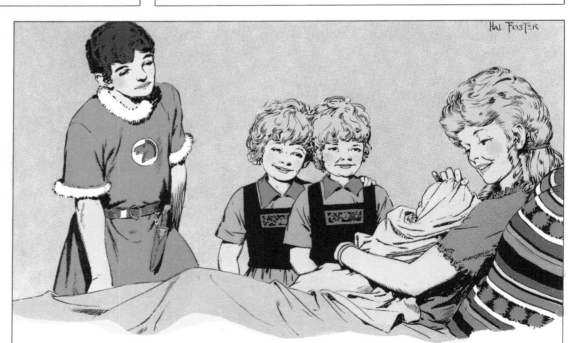

ALETA SHOULD BE CONTENT, FOR COURT LIFE IN CAMELOT IS BRIGHT AND GAY, HER FAMILY LOUD AND HEALTHY. BUT SHE IS LONELY. WHY BE MARRIED TO A GREAT BIG GORGEOUS HERO IF HE IS NOT AT ONE'S SIDE? SHE PLANS A PILGRIMAGE OF HER OWN.
NEXT WEEK - **Romance**
10-28-62

Prince Valiant
IN THE DAYS OF KING ARTHUR
WRITTEN AND ILLUSTRATED BY HAROLD R. FOSTER

Our Story: CAMELOT IS A GAY PLACE, BUT WITHOUT HER PRINCE VALIANT AT HER SIDE ALETA IS LONELY. SHE DREAMS OF THEIR GLORIOUS, ROMANTIC PAST; OF THE TIME SHE CAUSED A MINOR EXPLOSION BY USING THE SORCERY THAT SEEMS TO COME NATURALLY TO SMALL BLONDES WITH GREY EYES.

SHE HAD WAVED THOSE INCREDIBLY LONG LASHES UP AT HIM AND EARNED SOME CRUSHED RIBS AND A WHOLLY SATISFACTORY DECLARATION . . . .

. . . . . AND THAT TIME WHEN SHE HAD OVERDONE THE IMPUDENCE, AND HE HAD TOSSED HER INTO THE FISH POND! SUCH A MAN! WHAT A MAGNIFICENT BRUTE!

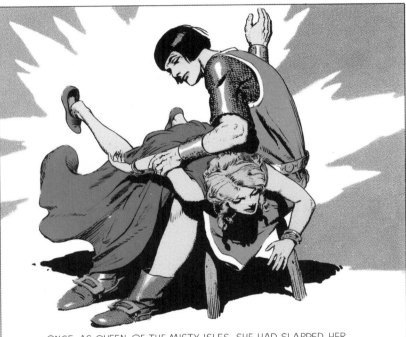

ONCE, AS QUEEN OF THE MISTY ISLES, SHE HAD SLAPPED HER FAVORITE SUBJECT. THAT WAS THE TIME HE HAD POINTED OUT SHARPLY THAT SHE WAS ALSO A WIFE. OH! ONE COULDN'T HELP LOVING SUCH A GORGEOUS CREATURE!

HE HAD BEEN GOOD TO HER IN OTHER WAYS TOO. JUST SO SHE WOULD NOT BE LONELY WHEN HE WENT ADVENTURING, HE HAD SURROUNDED HER WITH FOUR ACTIVE CHILDREN, THE DEAR.

ALETA EXPLODES INTO ACTION; "KATWIN, MIND THE CHILDREN WHILE I AM AWAY. ARN, GET READY TO RIDE, WE GO TO VISIT YOUR FATHER!"

1343.

ALETA IS A QUEEN, REPORTED TO BE QUITE PRETTY AND, THEREFORE, POSSESSED OF A LARGE AMOUNT OF VANITY. WHEN SHE HAS PACKED WHAT SHE CONSIDERS THE BARE NECESSITIES, IT TAKES MANY BAGGAGE ANIMALS TO CARRY THE LOAD.

NEXT WEEK- **The Safari**

11-4-62

Prince Valiant
IN THE DAYS OF KING ARTHUR
WRITTEN AND ILLUSTRATED BY HAROLD R FOSTER

Our Story: ALETA WEARIES OF COURT LIFE AND LONGS TO BE WITH PRINCE VALIANT ONCE MORE. HIS ABSENCE HAS MADE HER HEART GROW FONDER (NOT LOGICAL OF COURSE, BUT FEMININE). SHE TAKES ARN ALONG TO GIVE HIM EXPERIENCE.

BUT ARN HAS TRAVELED ALL THE WAY TO BAGDAD WITH HIS FATHER AND HAS LEARNED MUCH. IT IS HE WHO CHOOSES THE CAMPING PLACE WITH AN EYE TO WATER, GRAZING AND DEFENSE, POSTING SENTRIES AND SENDING OUT SCOUTS.

THE SCOUTS BRING BACK FRIGHTENING STORIES; SOME OF THE STARVING PILGRIMS LEARNED FIRST TO FORAGE FOR FOOD, THEN TO PILLAGE, AND FINALLY TO BECOME DANGEROUS GANGS OF ROBBERS.

ONLY BECAUSE THEY ARE WELL MOUNTED DID THEY ESCAPE CONTACT WITH SOME OF THESE GANGS. AT LAST A SCOUT TELLS THEM THAT THE NEXT DAY WILL SEE THE END OF THEIR JOURNEY. ALETA PREPARES FOR THE MEETING WITH ALL THE SKILL AT HER COMMAND.

THE MEETING IS FAR FROM ROMANTIC. VAL IS DOWN IN A MUDDY HOLE DIRECTING THE WORKERS, AND THERE IS LITTLE RESEMBLANCE TO A WARRIOR PRINCE.

HAL FOSTER

"OH, HUSBAND, YOU ARE SO BEAUTIFULLY DIRTY, SO HANDSOMELY SMUDGED!" SHE EXCLAIMS, "AND YOU HAVE PUT ON SO MUCH WEIGHT.....ALL MUD!"

NEXT WEEK- **To Save the Treasure**

1344

11-11-62

Prince Valiant
IN THE DAYS OF KING ARTHUR

WRITTEN AND ILLUSTRATED BY HAROLD R. FOSTER

Our Story: ALETA TIRES OF COURT LIFE AND MAKES A LONG JOURNEY TO BE ONCE MORE WITH PRINCE VALIANT. AND VAL HAS BEEN TOILING ON THE NEW CHURCH WITH SUCH ARDOR THAT HE HAS FORGOTTEN ABOUT HIS APPEARANCE.

ALETA'S PAVILION IS PUT UP ON A PLEASANT STREAMSIDE GROVE, AND VAL COLLECTS HIS BELONGINGS FROM THE LEAKY TENT HE HAS SHARED WITH WOJAN AND THE ABBOT.

FOR A BRIEF MOMENT VAL LOOKS BACK TO WHERE HE HAS LIVED THE SIMPLE LIFE, SLEEPING UNDER HIS CLOAK ON A BED OF DAMP RUSHES. WITH A SIGH HE TURNS TOWARD ALETA'S LUXURIOUS PAVILION.

ALETA SINGS GAILY AS SHE UNPACKS HER DAINTY THINGS, AND SOON THE TENT TAKES ON THE APPEARANCE OF AN ORIENTAL BAZAAR AND SMELLS LIKE A FLOWER GARDEN.

ALETA HAS NO HANDMAIDEN TO KEEP THINGS IN ORDER, AND VAL WATCHES HIS ARMS AND ARMOR DISAPPEAR UNDER A CLOUD OF BRIGHT SCARVES AND GOWNS. SOON NO ONE CAN FIND ANYTHING.

IN THE MUD-AND-WATTLE VILLAGE WHERE THE WORKERS ARE QUARTERED VAL FINDS TWO YOUNG WOMEN TO ACT AS MAIDS, AND HE IS FREE TO CONTINUE WORK ON THE CHURCH.

ONE DAY VAL AND ARN ARE STANDING HIGH ON THE SCAFFOLD AND VAL POINTS EASTWARD. *"THERE, WHERE THE MISTS HANG LOW, ARE THE FENS WHERE I SPENT MY BOYHOOD, A WILD AND BEAUTIFUL PLACE FULL OF MYSTERY AND ADVENTURE."* ARN IS SILENT AS HE GAZES INTO THE DISTANCE - MYSTERY! ADVENTURE!

NEXT WEEK—**Memories of the Past.**

1345.

11-18-62

HAL FOSTER

Prince Valiant
IN THE DAYS OF KING ARTHUR
WRITTEN AND ILLUSTRATED BY Harold R Foster

"...... AT FIRST I WAS CONFINED TO OUR ISLAND, BUT THE GREAT MARSH WITH ITS WINDING CHANNELS AND MYRIAD WATERFOWL CALLED FOR EXPLORATION......."

Our Story: TO THE EAST OF THEIR CAMP LIE THE MYSTERIOUS FENS WHERE PRINCE VALIANT SPENT HIS BOYHOOD. WITH ARN A SPELLBOUND LISTENER VAL RECOUNTS HIS EARLY ADVENTURES. "AFTER THE FJORDS AND MOUNTAINS OF THULE, THE FENS WERE LIKE ANOTHER WORLD........"

"...SO I CARVED A DUGOUT AND RANGED FAR AND WIDE..."

SKETCHES OF PRINCE VALIANT'S BOYHOOD REPRODUCED FROM ORIGINAL PAGE DONE IN 1937.

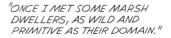

"ONCE I MET SOME MARSH DWELLERS, AS WILD AND PRIMITIVE AS THEIR DOMAIN."

"I SHOWED THEIR BOY HOW TO SPEAR THE GREAT PIKE."

"AND HE IN TURN TAUGHT ME TO SNARE WILDFOWL WITH A WEIGHTED NET. AS THE YEARS WENT BY I HAD MANY ADVENTURES. ONCE THE MUD RELEASED THE BONES OF A HUGE CREATURE THAT DWELT IN THE MARSH IN OLDEN TIMES."

ARN IS INTERESTED AND ASKS A THOUSAND QUESTIONS, AND IT IS FAR INTO THE NIGHT BEFORE HE IS SATISFIED.

1346.

VAL IS NOT SURPRISED WHEN NEXT DAY ARN HAS SECURED A CANOE AND ANNOUNCES THAT HE IS OFF FOR THE FENS. ALETA IS WORRIED, FOR THERE ARE MANY DANGERS AND ARN LOOKS SMALL, BUT VAL LAUGHS. "IT IS TIME HE LEARNED TO BE SELF-SUFFICIENT," HE SAYS.

NEXT WEEK-The Fens

11-25-62

Prince Valiant
IN THE DAYS OF KING ARTHUR
WRITTEN AND ILLUSTRATED BY HAROLD R FOSTER

Our Story : WHEN PRINCE VALIANT REALIZES THAT THE STREAM BY WHICH THEY ARE CAMPED RUNS INTO THE FENS, HE REGALES HIS SON ARN WITH STORIES OF THE ADVENTUROUS BOYHOOD HE SPENT THERE. ARN DOES NOT DELAY. NEXT DAY HE IS ON HIS WAY TO SEEK HIS OWN ADVENTURES.

AND IS NOT LONG IN LEARNING SOME THINGS ABOUT PUNTING.

BY MIDDAY HE IS IN THE GREAT MARSH, AND THE HILLS FADE AWAY IN THE DISTANCE.

TOWARD EVENING ARN DISCOVERS THE FENS ARE REALLY A MYSTERIOUS PLACE. THERE ARE DOZENS OF CHANNELS, LAKES, PONDS, WATER-MEADOWS. LOST! HE WONDERS IF HIS FATHER EVER FELT THE TOUCH OF FEAR HE NOW FEELS.

NIGHT HAS FALLEN ERE HE FINDS ANY SOLID GROUND, A QUAKING MUD-BAR. CLOUDS OF MOSQUITOES ARISE, AND THE NOISES OF THE NIGHT BEGIN. THERE ARE CRIES AND SCREAMS, WHISPERING, HEAVY SPLASHING AMONG THE REEDS.

DAWN IS NOT MUCH BETTER, FOR A HEAVY MIST ROLLS IN FROM THE DISTANT SEA. HE PUSHES ON AIMLESSLY, HOPING TO FIND A DEFINITE CHANNEL.

THE MISTS GIVE WAY TO A STEADY RAIN AND ARN HAS NOT ONLY FOUND A CHANNEL.....HE HAS FOUND DOZENS, LEADING IN ALL DIRECTIONS.

THAT EVENING HE FINDS AN ISLAND, THE END OF HIS PROVISIONS, AND THE BEGINNING OF PANIC!

NEXT WEEK- TideWater

1547.

12-2-62

Prince Valiant
IN THE DAYS OF KING ARTHUR

WRITTEN AND ILLUSTRATED BY HAROLD R FOSTER

Our Story: DAWN OF A STORMY DAY; THERE IS NO SUN TO SHOW A LOST BOY HIS DIRECTIONS; HIS PROVISIONS ARE ALL GONE. SCARED? YES, HE ADMITS IN SELF-CONTEMPT. THEN THE WHISTLE OF A FINCH AND THE CHATTER OF A SQUIRREL REMIND HIM THAT THERE MUST BE NUTS AND BERRIES ON THE ISLAND.

NOT MUCH OF A MEAL, BUT IT QUELLS HIS HUNGER AND CALMS HIS FEARS. HE TRIES TO REMEMBER THE THINGS HIS FATHER TOLD HIM ABOUT THIS FORLORN PLACE.

"FOLLOW THE CURRENT AND YOU REACH THE SEA. TO RETURN, GO AGAINST THE CURRENT," HIS FATHER SAID. BUT IS THERE ANY FLOW OF WATER IN ALL THIS WIDE MARSH?

IT IS WHILE HE IS TRYING TO ENTICE A LARGE PIKE TO HIS SPEAR WITH A BRIGHT LURE THAT HE REMEMBERS SOMETHING ELSE - *"THE SURFACE WATER MOVES WITH THE WIND, BUT THE WEEDS ON THE BOTTOM SWAY WITH THE CURRENT."*

SO ARN SPENDS THE REST OF THE DAY HUNTING AND FISHING. THEN HE BUILDS A MUD FIREPLACE IN HIS CANOE AND GATHERS FIREWOOD. IF HE CANNOT FIND ANOTHER ISLAND, HE CAN AT LEAST COOK HIS GAME.

NEXT DAY HE STARTS OFF BRISKLY, HOPING TO REACH LAND BY NIGHTFALL. BUT WHEN HE TAKES A DRINK, THE WATER IS SALT! TIDE-WATER! HE HAS BEEN PADDLING NOT UPSTREAM, BUT AGAINST THE INCOMING TIDE.

1348.

HE TURNS AROUND AND RETRACES HIS ROUTE. NIGHT FINDS ARN RIGHT BACK WHERE HE STARTED.

NOW PRINCE VALIANT HAS A PROBLEM. HE WANTS HIS SON TO BE SELF-RELIANT, BUT ARE THE MYSTERIOUS FENS TOO MUCH FOR THE LAD?

NEXT WEEK - **Thorg, the Monster**

12-9-62

Prince Valiant
IN THE DAYS OF KING ARTHUR
WRITTEN AND ILLUSTRATED BY HAROLD R FOSTER

Our Story: AT DAWN OF THE FIFTH DAY ARN STARTS OUT ONCE MORE TO FIND A WAY OUT OF THE VAST SWAMPLANDS.

PRINCE VALIANT, IN A BORROWED DUGOUT, IS ALSO ON HIS WAY. ARN MUST LEARN TO LOOK AFTER HIMSELF, BUT PERHAPS HE IS NOT READY FOR SUCH A TEST AS THIS.

THE FENS HAVE CHANGED; SOME LAKES ARE CHOKED WITH WEEDS, CHANNELS HAVE CHANGED THEIR COURSE. VAL MARKS HIS PASSAGE.

OUTCASTS AND FUGITIVES LURK HERE. WELL HE REMEMBERS HIS MEETING WITH THORG AND WONDERS IF THE MONSTER STILL LIVES HERE.

FATHER AND SON SLEEP TEN MILES APART, AND VAL SLEEPS UNCONCERNED, FOR HE HAS FORGOTTEN HOW SCARY THE FENS CAN BE FOR A SMALL BOY.

OCCASIONALLY HE SENDS A BUGLE NOTE ACROSS THE MARSH AND LISTENS FOR AN ANSWERING CALL.

HAL FOSTER

AT LAST VAL MEETS ARN. HE IS PEERING DOWN INTO THE WATER TO READ IN THE SWAYING WEEDS THE DIRECTION OF THE CURRENT. AND THERE, CROUCHING ABOVE HIM, IS THE SINISTER GRAY FORM OF THORG. NEXT WEEK- **The Gift**

1549   12-16-62

Prince Valiant
IN THE DAYS OF KING ARTHUR
WRITTEN AND ILLUSTRATED BY HAROLD R FOSTER

Our Story: A GREAT STILLNESS HANGS OVER THE MARSH AS THE HUGE GRAY FIGURE OF THORG CROUCHES TO LEAP UPON THE UNWARY BOY. BOTH LOOK UP AT THE SOUND OF PRINCE VALIANT'S QUIET VOICE: *"THORG! DO NOT ANGER ME AGAIN. REMEMBER WHAT HAPPENED THE LAST TIME."* THORG'S GROWL FADES INTO A FRIGHTENED WHINE.

"BUT WHEN YOU RECEIVED ME IN PEACE I GAVE YOU THE PRESENT OF A KNIFE, REMEMBER?" THORG'S DIM WITS STRUGGLE WITH THIS PROBLEM. AT LAST HE GURGLES WITH PLEASURE AND PRODUCES THE KNIFE.

IT HAS BEEN WHETTED DOWN TO A FRAGILE THINNESS. VAL TOSSES HIM HIS OWN SAXEKNIFE, AND IT IS RECEIVED WITH A JOYFUL WHIMPER. VAL SIGNALS TO ARN AND THEY PADDLE AWAY, LEAVING THE WILD CREATURE TO GLOAT OVER HIS TREASURE.

VAL SPENT HIS BOYHOOD HUNTING HERE. THE CALL OF THE WIDE MARSHES IS TOO MUCH TO BE IGNORED, SO HE AND ARN GO HUNTING TOGETHER.

THE YOUNG DUCKS ARE JUST BEGINNING TO FLY, AND DECOY READILY. TIME FLIES BY UNNOTICED.

1350.

THE HUNTERS RETURN TRIUMPHANT, FORGETTING ALL THEIR ADVENTURES IN THE PRIDE OF THEIR SKILL. BUT ALETA REMEMBERS A WEEK OF FEARFUL ANXIETY. *"YOU HEARTLESS BRUTES,"* SHE WAILS. VAL SHAKES HIS PUZZLED HEAD. THEY ARE BACK SAFELY. WHAT WAS THERE TO WORRY ABOUT? OH, THESE WOMEN!

NEXT WEEK- **Ethwald the businessman**

HAL FOSTER

12-23-62

Our Story: PRINCE VALIANT TAKES ALETA IN HIS ARMS. IT IS AN OLD REMEDY FOR TEARS. BUT HE WONDERS WHY SHE SHOULD WORRY SO WHEN HE AND ARN ARE IN DANGER. DOESN'T SHE TRUST THEM?

NOW IT IS TIME TO RETURN TO DUTY AT CAMELOT, AND WOJAN AND THE ABBOT ASK HIM TO CARRY OUT AN IMPORTANT MISSION.
"WHEN YOU LEAVE, SIR VALIANT, OUR TREASURE WILL NO LONGER BE SAFE," THE ABBOT EXPLAINS. "WE WISH YOU WOULD TAKE IT TO CAMELOT WITH YOU."

"REMNANTS OF THE PILGRIM HOST HAVE FORMED INTO LARGE BANDS AND STILL PILLAGE THE COUNTRYSIDE."

PROOF OF THIS IS NOT LONG IN COMING. SOME TRAVELERS HAVE A BRUSH WITH THESE OUTLAWS AND TAKE REFUGE IN THE HALF-FINISHED MONASTERY.

UNTIL THE KING SENDS A TROOP TO DISPERSE THESE RUFFIANS, THE LAND ROUTE TO CAMELOT WILL BE PERILOUS. VAL RIDES TO THE COAST AND CHARTERS A SHIP SO THEY CAN GO BY SEA.

WHEN HE RETURNS, THE TRAVELERS BEG TO TAKE PASSAGE WITH HIM AS FAR AS THEIR FIEF ON THE COAST NEAR HASTINGS.

1351.

VAL IS MORE INTENT ON THE PROPER CARE OF ARVAK THAN THE STOWAGE OF THE TREASURE. NOT SO HIS GUESTS......

12-30-62

.....THEIR LEADER, ETHWALD, RAISES HIS EYEBROWS AT THE SIGHT OF THE CHESTS. THEREAFTER HE SPENDS HIS TIME PLANNING FOR AN OPULENT FUTURE.
NEXT WEEK - The Quarry

Creo-Dipt roof and side-walls add beauty to this famous Music Box Cottage, designed by the T. H. Maenner Company, Omaha, Nebraska.

BEAUTY *that* PAYS *its* OWN WAY

YOU can give your new home the added beauty of Creo-Dipt Shingles and still save money. Even the *first* cost of Creo-Dipts is less than usual side-wall materials.

Or, you can re-beautify and *re-value* your old home by covering the old clapboards with Creo-Dipts. This costs you less than two re-paintings.

In either case you save money. One home owner figures that over a period of twenty years, his Creo-Dipts will cost him one-third as much as ordinary siding.

And for new roofs or for re-roofing, Creo-Dipt savings are just as startling as for side-walls.

Seldom can you get greater beauty at less cost. But this is true with Creo-Dipts, because year after year they save so much in upkeep. Write for details.

CREO-DIPT COMPANY, INC., 1101 OLIVER ST., NORTH TONAWANDA, N. Y.
In Canada: Creo-Dipt Company, Ltd., 1610 Royal Bank Bldg., Toronto

CREO-DIPT
Stained Shingles

Write for photographs!

If you wish to transform your old home—or if you plan to build—send 25c for interesting and helpful portfolio of actual photographs of Creo-Dipt houses designed by prominent architects.

Lumber dealers everywhere stock Creo-Dipts. Plants located for easy shipping at No. Tonawanda, Minneapolis, Kansas City, Mo., Vancouver, B. C. Sales offices in principal cities.

© C-D Co., Inc., 1926

HAL FOSTER'S ADVERTISING ART: HOME AND HEARTH

Compliled and Annotated by Brian M. Kane

Harold Rudolf "Hal" Foster always considered himself a second-tier advertising artist; he hoped to work for a prestigious firm one day. Most of the advertisements in this gallery are from 1925–1927, and represent a transitional time for Foster. If you look closely at Foster's signature on the Creo-Dipt and Wurlitzer illustrations, you will see the "JO" sigil after his name; but on the remaining images, when present, his signature is followed by the "PY" brand. The former indicates Foster's first employer in Chicago, the Jahn & Ollier engraving company, while the latter denotes the Palenske-Young advertising studio. In 1925, Reinhold Heinrich "Pal" Palenske left the firm he cofounded, and into that void walked Hal Foster. When you consider that some of the ads had to be completed months in advance, it is understandable that there is a delay in timing between Foster's entrance and the publication dates (Foster freelanced for Jahn & Ollier for years after his move). Some of the magazines that carried these Foster advertisements, such as *The Modern Priscilla*, only sold six-hundred thousand copies per month, while *The Saturday Evening Post* and *McCall's* both had monthly circulations exceeding two million copies (Peterson, p. 12 & p. 56). Even though these are modest illustrations by a fledging artist, Foster's trademark attention to detail is clearly evident. The Great Depression curtailed Foster's advertising dreams, and, while it is difficult to find a silver lining to the worst economic disaster of the twentieth century, without that happening *Prince Valiant* would never have graced the color Sunday comics pages.

Opposite: *Creo-Dipt advertisement for the January 9, 1926* The Saturday Evening Post, *p. 149.*

Right: *Kalamazoo Stove advertisement from the August 1930 issue of* The Country Gentleman.

REFERENCE

Peterson, Theodore (1956). *Magazines in the Twentieth Century.* Urbana: The University of Illinois Press.

Pretty Clothes *and* Brighter Homes
– at your finger tips

THE magic of home-dyeing! It's almost like having a wishing-ring, when you want a bright, new dress. Or a change in the color-scheme of drapes and hangings, throughout the house. You can have these things overnight! And *all for a few cents.*

You can home-dye anything, easy as you could wash it. The result is always perfect, if you always use true dyes. There's nothing to good dyeing except to use good dyes. Diamond dyes will dye any material, all the standard colors and new shades right over the old. Or do the most gorgeous tinting in delicate, true tones.

Mrs. Martin will help you

A Home Service department offers every user of Diamond dyes practical advice and assistance. It is in charge of Mrs. Martin, who will gladly help you in the choice of colors, matching any special shade, or the best way to dye or tint anything. Write her any question about dyeing anything in your wardrobe, the children's clothes, batik work, etc.

Take the old, yellow dress from the closet—and make it a smart copper brown! With the same Diamond dyes, tint your scarf and stockings to match it.

Are you tired of your faded pink waist? Diamond dye it a rich Gipsy red. Or the blue waist that is too dull; change it to some brilliant shade like parrot green.

Why not have new curtains this Fall—without buying a yard of material! Diamond dyes give any shade you can find at the draper's. And color table covers and bedspreads to harmonize with the hangings. Think of the sewing you save—and the *money*—by home-dyeing!

The Secret of Beautiful Dyeing and Tinting

There's nothing to learn about dyeing. The skill is all i[n] the dyes. The one thing required is *real dye.* And the sam[e] is true of tinting. Only real dyes can tint in even, true tone[s] like the sheer fabrics have when bought. Don't streak you[r] fine lingerie with the synthetic coloring matter now offere[d] in various forms! The original Diamond dyes (standard fo[r] fifty years) are sold by every drug store in the U. S. A[nd] for only 15 cents!

Big Dye and Tint Book Free!

A valuable book Color Craft free and postpaid, if yo[u] write. Full of pictures and suggestions for dyeing dozen[s] of things at home. To be sure of a copy, clip thi[s] coupon now:

DIAMOND DYES
Burlington, Vermont

Please send Color Craft, the big illustrated book on home dyeing and tinting, free.

Name..

Address...

Town........................... *State*.......................

Diamond Dyes
Make it NEW for 15 cents

For Personal Attention
to your problems of color, style, etc—

Opposite: *Hal Foster's wife, Helen, may have been the model for this Diamond Dyes advertisement, which appeared in the November 1926 McCall's magazine.*

The style of these three Foster pen-and-ink images, from Diamond Dyes' 1926 Color Craft catalog, appears to be highly influenced by the work of popular, early-nineteenth century illustrator Franklin Booth.

J. A. Rustin
Forty-nine Years With Diamond Dyes

Top: *This ad, for a French Renaissance Design piano from Wurlitzer's Period Grands collection, appeared in the February 1926* The House Beautiful.

Bottom: *The Jacobean Design piano (from the same collection) was advertised in the May 1926* The House Beautiful.

While these illustrations appeared a decade before Prince Valiant *premiered, it is interesting to see elements of romance and myth in the paintings behind the pianos. Could that be Sir Lancelot du Lac behind the French Renaissance piano? And who is that longhaired blonde strolling through the woods behind the Jacobean Art Grand? As Charles Vess points out in this volume's foreword, "We are all the sum of the stories we have been told." It appears to have been true for Foster as well.*

Opposite: *This ad for the Spanish Design piano, also from Wurlitzer's Period Grands collection, ran in the November 1925* The House Beautiful.

WURLITZER ⌢ PERIOD ⌢ GRANDS

YOU see it. You hear it. You want it. You buy it! Then ever after, the perfect blending of its true design with your other furnishings and the pure, rich loveliness of its tone, are a never-ending joy. There are Wurlitzer Period Grands in fifteen authentic designs—each, with or without the standard Apollo reproducing action. They range in price upwards from $875—terms most attractive. At all Wurlitzer stores and from leading dealers everywhere.

WURLITZER GRAND PIANO CO., DE KALB, ILL.

Principal Wurlitzer Stores

NEW YORK	BUFFALO	CLEVELAND	CHICAGO	CINCINNATI	ST. LOUIS	SAN FRANCISCO	LOS ANGELES
120 W. 42nd St.	674 Main St.	1017 Euclid Ave.	329 S. Wabash Ave.	121 E. Fourth St.	1006 Olive St.	250 Stockton St.	814 S. Broadway

Louis XIV Design

Jacobean Design

WURLITZER
REG. U.S. PAT. OFF.
SPANISH DESIGN
Illustrated Above

Italian Renaissance

These photos are of Hal's sons Edward Lusher "Teddy" Foster II (the taller of the two) and Arthur James Foster. In 1925, Foster's boys were nine and six years old, respectively. Just compare their clothes to these Jelke Margarine advertisements, and you can see why Foster did not have to go too far for inspiration—or models.

Energy Food for Active Bodies.

Sandwiches for the School Lunch Box

for recipes see page 13

Top Right: *A 1927* Jelke Margarine *catalog illustration, p. 4.*

Bottom Left: *Jelke Margarine advertisement from a 1927* Modern Priscilla *magazine.*

HEALTH
in every tempting bite

Give your children plenty of Jelke GOOD LUCK Margarine and bread to create energy, stimulate growth and build firm flesh and sturdy bones. Made of 3 of Nature's most healthful and appetizing fats, GOOD LUCK is rich in nourishment and has that delicately delicious flavor you usually associate only with costly spreads-for-bread. Yet it's so very inexpensive that you can use it generously, not only on the table but in cooking and baking, too. Try it!

Most good dealers sell GOOD LUCK

JELKE
GOOD LUCK
MARGARINE

The Finest Spread for Bread

JOHN F. JELKE CO.
GOOD LUCK
OLEOMARGARINE

Send this coupon and 10c to John F. Jelke Co., 759 S. Washtenaw Ave., Chicago, for 40-page illustrated book containing 75 new recipes for cakes, icings, pies, hot breads, cookies, puddings, sauces, sandwiches, etc.

Name
Address

More than a delicious spread

,, it creates strength and energy ,,

Nothing uses up a boy's energy quite so fast as strenuous sports like football. Therefore it's important these crisp, Fall days to give him an energy-creating food which he will eat because he *likes* it . . . both at meals and in-between.

Jelke GOOD LUCK Margarine is just such a food. Made of fresh, wholesome ingredients, it's not only a supremely delicious spread for bread but one of the very best energy foods known to food authorities.

So wonderfully tempting is the flavor of GOOD LUCK that it actually causes children to eat more bread. Thus, in addition to its own wealth of nourishment, your youngsters get more of the invaluable food elements so lavishly contained in wheat.

Most good dealers carry GOOD LUCK. Ask for it at yours. You'll be pleased to find how delicious it is . . . and how very little it costs. Use it in all your cooking and baking, too!

JELKE
GOOD LUCK
MARGARINE
The Finest Spread for Bread

THIS new and different cook book tells how to give your cooking and baking that rich, appetizing flavor at low cost.

Send this coupon and 10c to John F. Jelke Co., 759 S. Washtenaw Ave., Chicago, for 40-page illustrated book containing 75 new recipes for cakes, icings, pies, hot breads, cookies, puddings, sauces, sandwiches, etc.

Name_____

Address_____
_____

This Jelke Margarine advertisement ran in a 1927 Modern Priscilla *magazine.*

Heads of Families, too

"have "taken up" making Thompson's Chocolate

"DOUBLE MALTED"
MALTED MILK *at home*

The head of a large corporation stood looking as wistfully as a small boy outside a circus tent, at a natty soda-clerk who was doing his stuff. "I always wanted to be a soda-clerk," he said sadly, "behind the counter mixing nifty drinks for soft eyed girls and big eyed kids. I never wanted to be in this d— packing business."

Now at Last

Now Thompson's has made it possible for anyone to make a genuine, "real professional" Chocolate Malted Milk at home. And do it in fifteen seconds.

By a secret process Thompson's has produced a "DOUBLE MALTED" Malted Milk that dissolves immediately. All you do is put two spoonfuls into a shaker or mason jar, pour in the milk and shake for fifteen seconds.

There Are 30 Glasses in Every Pound

You can get Thompson's Chocolate Flavored in one and five-pound packages. With five-pound cans, you get a big 75c full pint solid aluminum shaker free.

Sleep or Energy

In the secret process of making Thompson's, the vitamins are not destroyed and the activity of the enzymes which help to digest other foods is maintained. Thompson's not only digests itself, but digests many times its own weight in other foods. That is why a glassful during the day gives you almost instant energy while at bedtime it gives you rest and sleep.

Get Thompson's today at any grocer's or druggist's, or, if you prefer, mail the coupon for the biggest coupon value we have ever offered.

At the
Soda Fountain

Your soda fountain man deserves special credit for paying a bit more for Thompson's "DOUBLE MALTED" Malted Milk so as to serve you with an extra quality malted milk drink. Look for the Thompson's serving jar at the soda fountain.

Thompson's
"DOUBLE MALTED"
Sweet Chocolate Flavor
Malted Milk

30 real "professional" Chocolate MALTED MILKS *for* 60¢

Thompson's Malted Food Co.
Dept. 240—Waukesha, Wis.
Gentlemen:—

☐ Please send me your solid aluminum Individual Shaker large enough for one serving and a 3-day sample package of Thompson's Sweet Chocolate Flavored "DOUBLE MALTED" Malted Milk for which I enclose 25c.

OR

☐ Please send me your 3-day sample package (without shaker) for which I enclose 10c.

Name..

Street..City..................

IF IT'S THOMPSON'S IT'S "DOUBLE MALTED"

Don't
buck the bumps!

Like mean horses are cars without rebound controls. WEED Levelizers tame the roughest ride—they keep springs from snapping you up—they give you *riding comfort.*

And on good roads, Levelizers will *not* stiffen up your springs. Your balloon tire cushioning and soft spring action is still there—unmolested.

Order Levelizers for your car. Your dealer or garage man has them, or he can get them for you.

Use

WEED
Levelizers

"They level the road as you go"

AMERICAN CHAIN COMPANY, INC.
BRIDGEPORT, CONNECTICUT
In Canada
Dominion Chain Co., Limited, Niagara Falls, Ontario
DISTRICT SALES OFFICES: Boston, Chicago, New York, Philadelphia, Pittsburgh, San Francisco

Makers of WEED Chains *and* WEED Bumpers

Left: *This ad for Thompson's chocolate "Double Malted" milk ran in the August 20, 1927* The Saturday Evening Post, *p. 144.*

Right: *This Weed Chain ad ran in the August 28, 1926* The Saturday Evening Post, *p. 94.*

IN OUR NEXT VOLUME:

PRINCE VALIANT

VOL. 14: 1963–1964

Wars and rumors of wars: Prince Valiant finds himself drawn into battles both large and small, while Mordred plots a scandal that will shatter the bonds of the Fellowship of the Round Table. Saxons attack in the Battle of Baddon Hill, and the only one who can save King Arthur and the Knights of Camelot is Val's son, Prince Arn. In Thule, a guerilla war is waged against Val's father, King Aguar. Comics writer Roger Stern, in his foreword, looks at the artists inspired by Hal Foster.